Connect *with* English

GRAMMAR GUIDE 4

Kathleen F. Flynn • Marilyn Rosenthal • Irwin Feigenbaum • Linda Butler

with contributions by
Michael Berman • Robin Longshaw

Mc
Graw
Hill

Boston, Massachusetts   Burr Ridge, Illinois   Dubuque, Iowa   Madison, Wisconsin
New York, New York   San Francisco, California   St. Louis, Missouri
Bangkok   Bogotá   Caracas   Lisbon   London   Madrid   Mexico City
Milan   New Delhi   Seoul   Singapore   Sydney   Taipei   Toronto

McGraw-Hill

A Division of The McGraw·Hill Companies

CONNECT WITH ENGLISH: GRAMMAR GUIDE BOOK 4

This book is printed on acid-free paper.

domestic 1 2 3 4 5 6 7 8 9 0 QPD QPD 3 2 1 0 9 8
international 1 2 3 4 5 6 7 8 9 0 QPD QPD 3 2 1 0 9 8

ISBN 0-07-292771-2

Editorial director: Thalia Dorwick
Publisher: Tim Stookesberry
Development editor: Pam Tiberia
Marketing manager: Tracy Landrum
Production supervisor: Richard DeVitto
Print materials consultant: Marilyn Rosenthal
Project manager: Shannon McIntyre, Function Thru Form, Inc.
Design and Electronic Production: Function Thru Form, Inc.
Typeface: Frutiger
Printer and Binder: Quebecor Press Dubuque

Grateful acknowledgment is made for use of the following:

Still photography: Jeffrey Dunn, Ron Gordon, Judy Mason, Margaret Storm

Library of Congress Catalog Card No.: 97-75579

When ordering this title, use ISBN 0-07-115914-2.

TABLE OF CONTENTS

TO THE TEACHER

The primary goal of each *Grammar Guide* is to help students develop mastery of the grammatical structures found throughout the **Connect with English** video episodes. This introduction and the following visual tour provide important information on how each *Grammar Guide* and the corresponding video episodes can be successfully combined to teach English as a second or foreign language.

PROFICIENCY LEVEL:

Designed for beginning through high-intermediate students, *Grammar Guides 1-4* provide a systematic presentation of the basic structures and grammatical features of American English. Examples from the video episodes are used to illustrate grammatical structures in both presentation and practice.

Students at various proficiency levels can benefit from using the *Grammar Guides*. Lower-level students will find the *Grammar Guides* a valuable resource tool they can rely on to help them internalize the authentic language of the video. More advanced students will welcome the carefully sequenced review of the language and its connection to the video through numerous examples and practices.

LANGUAGE SKILLS

Grammar Guides 1-4 provide practice with the linguistic building blocks of the language. They give students an opportunity to analyze and review the structures through clear and simple grammar charts and explanations. Exercises are transparent and help students build from a receptive understanding of the grammar point to language production through controlled exercises and finally, free-writing, using the grammar point to talk about their own lives. The grammar charts and explanations are particularly helpful to students whose learning style relies on analysis and explanation. The opportunities for practice are useful to students who learn language inductively through observation and practice with the structures.

OPTIONS FOR USE

Each *Grammar Guide* can be used in a variety of different learning environments, including classroom, distance learning, tutorial, and/or independent study situations. Students can use *Grammar Guides 1-4* before or after they watch the corresponding video episode, to either preview or review critical structures and grammatical topics.

Grammar Guides 1-4 can easily be combined with other corresponding texts in the **Connect with English** print program. For classes with an emphasis on listening, *Video Comprehension Books 1-4* help students build listening comprehension skills and gain a clear understanding of the characters and story line in the video series. For classes with an emphasis on oral communication skills, *Conversation Books 1-4* contain a variety of pair, group, team, and whole-class activities based on important themes and events from each episode. Finally, there are 16 *Connections Readers* that offer students graded reading practice based on the **Connect with English** story. These readers also use the same grammatical scope and sequence found in *Grammar Guides 1-4*.

A VISUAL TOUR

This visual tour is designed to introduce the key features of *Grammar Guide 4*. The primary focus of each *Grammar Guide* is to help students develop mastery of key grammatical structures and concepts. *Grammar Guide 4* corresponds to episodes 37-48 of *Connect with English*. The scope and sequence of the grammar points in this book are developmental; topics become more advanced as the chapters progress.

Grammar Charts
The **Grammar Chart** explains the grammar topic and acts as a model that students can refer to as they do the exercises.

Photos
Photos from the corresponding video episode are used to illustrate the meaning of the grammar point.

Notes
The **Notes** section offers additional explanations about the material being presented. These sections have been carefully worded so that the language of instruction is no more advanced than the grammatical structures being presented in the text.

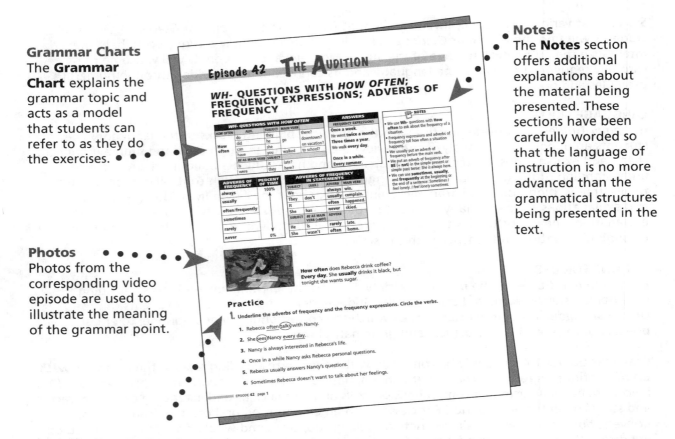

Contextualized Exercises
The first exercise in the **Practice** section is always based on the characters, situations, and events that happen in the video. This first exercise is also usually on the receptive level, allowing students to recognize the structural point before they actually need to produce it.

Chapter Structure

Every episode of *Grammar Guide 4* presents three grammar points, each on a two-page spread. Each grammar presentation has the following features:

- A grammar chart, illustrating the structures or grammatical features;
- Simple explanatory usage notes;
- A photo from the video episode illustrating the context of the grammar point;
- A practice section of exercises taking the student from a receptive knowledge to productive practice with the structure;
- A more advanced practice (**Power Practice**) section providing the student with an opportunity for free writing about his/her own life using the target structure.

Guided Practice

Subsequent exercises in the **Practice** section provide students with an opportunity to further practice the structure. The task in each exercise increases slightly in difficulty throughout each lesson. Some of these exercises are focused on the video, and others are set in other real-world contexts. The language used in all exercises — in direction lines, examples, and the items themselves — is very simple and utilizes only the structures that have been introduced up to that point in the book.

Relating Grammar to Everyday Life
The **Power Practice** section allows a chance for students to use the target structure to write about things that are meaningful in their own lives. It's a particularly useful tool for multilevel classrooms, as it gives students an opportunity to produce language at a variety of different levels.

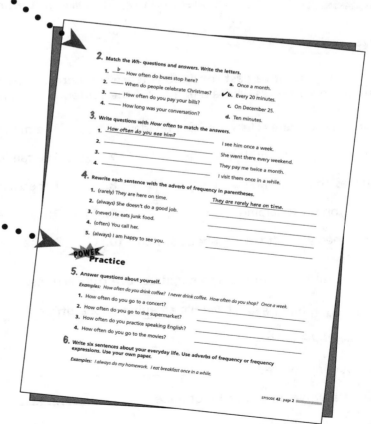

Episode 37 THANKSGIVING

REVIEW: PAST CONTINUOUS TENSE, AFFIRMATIVE AND NEGATIVE STATEMENTS

AFFIRMATIVE STATEMENTS		
SUBJECT	WAS/WERE	MAIN VERB + -ING
I He She It	was	working.
We You They	were	

NEGATIVE STATEMENTS		
SUBJECT	WAS/WERE + NOT	MAIN VERB + -ING
I He She It	was not wasn't	working.
We You They	were not weren't	

NOTES
- We use the past continuous tense for actions in progress in the past.
- We use [subject + auxiliary verb **was/were** (+ **not**) + simple form of main verb + **-ing**] for past continuous tense statements.

Brendan **was drinking** coffee.

Michael and Kevin **were eating**.

The men **were talking**. They **weren't working** in the kitchen.

Practice

1. Write **A** next to affirmative past continuous tense sentences. Write **N** next to negative past continuous tense sentences. Write a line (—) if the sentence is not in the past continuous tense.

1. __A__ The Caseys were celebrating the holiday.
2. __N__ They were not working.
3. __—__ It was Thanksgiving Day.
4. ____ Everyone was helping.
5. ____ The men weren't talking about Boston.
6. ____ The men were watching a football game.
7. ____ The family sat down to dinner together.
8. ____ Rebecca and Kevin weren't arguing.
9. ____ They were sitting next to each other.
10. ____ Michael made a toast.

2. Change the affirmative sentences to negative. Use contractions.

1. I was sleeping in the office. _I wasn't sleeping in the office._
2. They were drinking coffee. _____
3. She was working for free. _____
4. The refrigerator was making a lot of noise. _____
5. We were reading the book. _____

3. Complete the sentences with verbs from the box. Use the past continuous tense. Use contractions in the negative sentences.

call	clean	eat	listen	pay	ring	run	sing	talk	work

Affirmative Sentences

1. She __was calling__ her mother.

2. They _____ the house.

3. The thieves _____ from the police.

4. The phone _____ all day.

5. The student _____ to the teacher.

Negative Sentences

6. The computers __weren't working__.

7. He _____ enough fruit.

8. They _____ to me.

9. The actress _____ well.

10. I _____ the bills.

Practice

POWER

4. What were you doing each night last week at 9:00 p.m.? Write sentences in the past continuous tense.

Example: *Monday: I was doing my homework at 9:00 p.m.*

Monday: _____

Tuesday: _____

Wednesday: _____

Thursday: _____

Friday: _____

Saturday: _____

Sunday: _____

5. PRETEND: Write the beginning of a story. Write a description with at least six sentences in the past continuous tense.

Example: *It was raining again. A man was running down the dark street.*

_____

_____

_____

_____

_____

_____

REVIEW: PAST CONTINUOUS TENSE, *YES/NO* QUESTIONS AND SHORT ANSWERS; *WH-* QUESTIONS AND ANSWERS

YES/NO QUESTIONS		
WAS/WERE	**SUBJECT**	**MAIN VERB + -ING**
Was	I he she it	**helping**?
Were	we you they	

AFFIRMATIVE SHORT ANSWERS		
YES	**SUBJECT**	**WAS/WERE**
Yes,	I he she it	**was**.
	we you they	**were**.

NEGATIVE SHORT ANSWERS		
NO	**SUBJECT**	**WAS/WERE + NOT**
No,	I he she it	**was not.** **wasn't.**
	we you they	**were not.** **weren't.**

WH- QUESTIONS				
WH- QUESTION WORD	**WAS/WERE**	**SUBJECT**	**MAIN VERB + -ING**	
Who **Whom**	were	you	discussing?	
What	was	she	doing	there?
When	were	they	looking	for me?
Where	was	it	snowing?	

ANSWERS
Jack.
Shopping.
All morning.
In the mountains.

 NOTES
- We use [auxiliary verb **Was/Were** + subject + simple form of main verb + **-ing**] for **Yes/No** questions in the past continuous tense.
- Short answers in the past continuous tense are like short answers with **BE** in the simple past tense.
- We use [**Wh-** question word + auxiliary verb **was/were** + subject + simple form of main verb + **-ing**] for information questions in the past continuous tense.
- We use **Who** in conversation and in informal writing. We use **Whom** in formal writing and in formal speaking.

Was Rebecca **singing** a traditional song?
Yes, she **was**.

Who was she **singing** it for?
The whole family.

Practice

6. Check (✔) the questions in the past continuous tense.

1. ✔ Were Kevin and Michael talking?

2. _____ What were they talking about?

3. _____ What did Peggy ask Rebecca?

4. _____ What was Rebecca singing?

5. _____ Was she singing her own music?

6. _____ Where were Kevin and Rebecca walking?

7. _____ Did they go into the barn?

8. _____ Were they talking about their mother?

9. _____ Did Kevin remember her?

10. _____ Was Rebecca thinking about San Francisco?

7. Complete the **Yes/No** questions with your own words. Use the past continuous tense. Complete the short answers. Use contractions in negative short answers.

1. __Were__ you __taking__ a photo?   Yes, __I was.__

2. _____ the bird _____ a lot?   No, _____

3. _____ the players _____ the game?   Yes, _____

4. _____ the waiter _____ the food?   Yes, _____

5. _____ the woman _____ a red dress?   No, _____

8. Answer the questions with short answers. Use contractions in negative short answers.

1. Were you talking at age two? __Yes, I was. (or) No, I wasn't.__

2. Were you and your friends learning English at age 10? _____

3. Was your father working at age 15? _____

4. Was your mother working at age 15? _____

5. Were you driving a car at age 14? _____

9. Write **Wh-** questions. Use the past continuous tense. Write answers. Use your own words.

1. who / you / call   __Who were you calling? My mother.__

2. what / he / do / to the car   _____

3. where / she / practice   _____

4. who / you / talk / to   _____

5. what / they / make / for dinner   _____

POWER **Practice**

10. Ask your friends or classmates about their lives at age 13. Write four **Yes/No** questions and four **Wh-** questions for them in the past continuous tense. Use your own paper.

Examples: *Were you going to school? Where were you living at age 13?*

11. PRETEND: Your friend was out last night doing something unusual. Write four **Yes/No** and four **Wh-** questions for your friend about his/her activities. Use the past continuous tense. Use your own paper.

Examples: *Were you singing at a concert? Who were you talking to?*

REVIEW: PAST CONTINUOUS TENSE AND SIMPLE PAST TENSE

PAST CONTINUOUS TENSE	
They **were watching** TV	while I **was making** dinner.
SIMPLE PAST TENSE	
I **made** dinner,	and then we **ate**.
PAST CONTINUOUS TENSE	**SIMPLE PAST TENSE**
While I **was making** dinner,	the phone **rang**.
I **was making** dinner	when the phone **rang**.

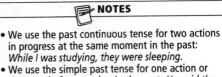

NOTES

- We use the past continuous tense for two actions in progress at the same moment in the past: *While I was studying, they were sleeping.*
- We use the simple past tense for one action or situation before another in the past: *He paid the bill, and they left.*
- We use the past continuous tense and the simple past tense for an interruption. One action was taking place when another took place: *While we were shopping, I met an old friend.*

While Brendan **was driving** Rebecca to the airport, she **asked** him about her father.

Practice

12. Check (✔) the sentences that show an interruption. These sentences have verbs in both the past continuous tense and the simple past tense.

1. __✔__ While Brendan was driving, Rebecca asked about his relationship with her father.

2. _____ Brendan stopped the truck, and he told her the story.

3. _____ When Brendan went away to war as a young man, he was dating Margaret Kelly.

4. _____ He asked his brother to look after his new girlfriend.

5. _____ While Brendan was fighting in the war, Patrick and Margaret fell in love.

6. _____ They got married while Brendan was serving in the army in Korea.

13. Write *1* next to the action already in progress when an interruption took place. Underline the verb.

1. _____ When the phone rang, __1__ we <u>were watching</u> TV.

2. _____ While we were taking a walk, _____ it started to rain.

3. _____ My friends were eating _____ when I got to the restaurant.

4. _____ When you called, _____ I was taking a shower.

5. _____ While she was sleeping, _____ she had a strange dream.

6. _____ The sun came out _____ while we were playing.

14. Circle the correct tense.

1. He called while we talked / (were talking) about him.

2. The fire started / was starting while everyone was sleeping.

3. He moved / was moving furniture when he hurt his back.

4. She was living in Los Angeles when he met / was meeting her.

5. We were driving south on Main St. when we saw / were seeing the accident.

6. I took / was taking a shower when somebody knocked on the door.

15. Combine the two sentences. Use *while* or *when*.

1. I was watching TV. I fell asleep. _While I was watching TV, I fell asleep._

2. He was skiing. He broke his leg. _He was skiing when he broke his leg._

3. We were washing the car. We got very wet. _____

4. I was shopping. I found the perfect shoes. _____

5. She was listening to the radio. She heard the good news. _____

6. I was riding on the bus. I saw you on your bicycle. _____

POWER Practice

16. Complete the following sentences about interruptions in your past. Use the simple past tense for the interruption.

Example: While I was studying, I heard a loud noise outside in the street.

1. While I was studying, _____

2. While I was eating dinner, _____

3. _____ while I was taking a shower.

4. When I was sleeping, _____

5. _____ while I was trying to do my work.

17. Write six sentences that show an interruption by using the simple past tense with the past continuous tense. Use *when* or *while*. Write about you or your family or friends. Use your own paper.

Examples: I was sleeping when my alarm rang this morning.
My parents met while they were working at the same place.

STARTING OVER

REVIEW: *WH-* QUESTIONS WITH *WHO, WHAT, WHEN, WHERE, WHY,* AND *HOW LONG*

WH- QUESTIONS				
WH- QUESTION WORD	AUX.	SUBJECT	MAIN VERB	
Who Whom	did	you	see	there?
What	does	he	do?	
When	can	they	help	us?
Where	are	you	going?	
Why	was	she	singing?	
How long	will	they	be	away?

ANSWERS
All our friends.
He's an engineer.
Saturday.
Downtown.
She was happy.
One year.

NOTES

- We usually use [**Wh-** question word or phrase + auxiliary verb + subject + main verb] for information questions.
- We use [**Wh-** question word or phrase + main verb **BE** + subject] for information questions with **BE** in the simple present or simple past tense.
- We use auxiliary verbs in combination with main verbs.
- We can use forms of **BE** as auxiliary verbs and as main verbs.
- The abbreviation **AUX.** = auxiliary verb.

WH- QUESTIONS WITH *BE*: SIMPLE PRESENT AND SIMPLE PAST TENSES			
WH- QUESTION WORD	BE	SUBJECT	
Who	are	those girls?	
What	is	the capital?	
When	is	Christmas?	
Where	was	the class?	
Why	were	you	late?
How long	was	the movie?	

ANSWERS
My cousins.
Paris.
December 25.
In Room 221.
Because of traffic.
Two hours.

Where did Rebecca **go**?
Back to Nancy's house.

Practice

1. Match the *Wh-* questions and answers.

1. __e__ Where did Rebecca go?

2. _____ How long was Rebecca away?

3. _____ What do Rebecca and Nancy talk about?

4. _____ Why is Edward unhappy?

5. _____ Who does Alberto invite to the opera?

a. Rebecca's trip and Nancy's uncle, Edward.

b. Rebecca.

c. Because he can't come home.

d. A few weeks.

✔ **e.** Back to San Francisco.

2. Put the words in order. Write *Wh-* questions.

1. did / see / where / you / movie / the

   Where did you see the movie?

2. she / who / does / with / study

   _____

3. school / you / do / did / at / what / today

   _____

4. will / when / me / you / call

   _____

5. they / stay / did / there / how long

   _____

3. Write *Wh-* questions about the underlined information from the story.

1. Rebecca is living <u>at Nancy's house in San Francisco.</u>

   Where is Rebecca living?

2. She goes to school <u>at The San Francisco College of Music.</u> _____

3. She missed a lot of classes <u>because her father died.</u> _____

4. Her father died <u>a little while ago.</u> _____

5. She stayed at her uncle's farm <u>for a short time.</u> _____

6. Rebecca needs to call <u>her college advisor.</u> _____

4. Write a *Wh-* question for each answer. Use your imagination.

1. Where do you want to go? _____   Hawaii.

2. _____   Because I was sleeping.

3. _____   A rich man.

4. _____   As soon as possible.

5. _____   For six months.

6. _____   A check for $1,000,000.

Practice

5. PRETEND: Your friend just came back from a trip. Write six *Wh-* questions for your friend about this trip. Use *Who, What, When, Where, Why,* and *How long.* Use your own paper.

Examples: Where did you stay? When did you get home?

6. PRETEND: Your friend is starting a new job soon. Write six *Wh-* questions for your friend about the job. Use your own paper.

Examples: When did you get this job? What will you do there?

WH- QUESTIONS: *WHO/WHAT* AS SUBJECTS; *WHO/WHOM/WHAT* AS OBJECTS

WHO/WHAT AS SUBJECTS

WHO/WHAT	VERB	
Who	is	in the car?
	can play	the piano?
What	is happening	there?
	caused	the problem?

WHO/WHOM/WHAT AS OBJECTS

	WHO/WHOM/WHAT	AUX.	SUBJECT	MAIN VERB
R E V I E W	Who Whom	did	you	call?
		are	they	discussing?
		will	we	invite?
	What	does	he	want?
		can	we	do?
		was	she	cooking?

NOTES

- We use [**Who/What** + verb] for information questions about the subject.
- We use [**Who/Whom/What** + auxiliary verb + subject + main verb] for information questions about the object.
- We can use **Who** or **Whom** in questions about the object. We use **Who** in conversation and in informal writing. We use **Whom** in formal writing and in formal speaking.
- **AUX.** = auxiliary verb.

Who did Rebecca **call** when she came back?
Her advisor.

Practice

7. Write **S** next to questions with **Who** or **What** as the subject. Write **O** next to questions with **Who**, **Whom**, or **What** as the object.

1. __S__ Who made some tea for Rebecca?

2. __O__ Who did Rebecca call?

3. _____ What did her advisor say?

4. _____ Who called Emma Washington?

5. _____ Who looks at Patrick's photo?

6. _____ Whom does Rebecca tell about Brendan?

7. _____ What was Rebecca planning?

8. _____ What caused the problem between Nancy and Patrick?

8. Complete the **Wh-** questions with **Who** or **What** as the subject.

1. ___Who___ is at the door?

2. _____ happened last night at 9:30?

3. _____ wore a funny costume?

4. _____ belongs to him?

5. _____ can play the guitar?

6. _____ is the answer?

9. Put the words in order. Write **Wh-** questions.

1. you / for / what / have / lunch / did

   What did you have for lunch? _____

2. is / for / working / she / who

   _____

3. buy / what / he / her / did / for

   _____

4. can / do / after / I / what / lunch

   _____

5. does / want / who / she / see / to

   _____

6. were / what / they / there / doing

   _____

10. Read the answers. Write questions with **Who** or **What** about the underlined information.

1. What did you buy? _____   I bought a new hat.

2. Who called you last night? _____   Lee called me last night.

3. _____   Her address is 65 Maple Street.

4. _____   Bob is coming for dinner.

5. _____   He lives with his wife and kids.

6. _____   They brought food to the beach.

7. _____   An accident caused the traffic jam.

POWER Practice

11. PRETEND: You are going to ask people questions about housework. Write eight questions for your survey. Use **Who** or **What**.

Examples: Who cooks for your family? What should children do in the house?

1. _____

2. _____

3. _____

4. _____

5. _____

6. _____

7. _____

8. _____

WH- QUESTIONS WITH *WHAT/WHICH/ HOW MUCH/HOW MANY (+ NOUN)*

WH- QUESTION WORDS AS ADJECTIVES		
WH- QUESTION WORD	**NOUN**	
What	cities	did they visit?
Which	tie	looks better with this shirt?
How much	time	do we have?
How many	students	are in your class?

WH- QUESTION WORDS AS PRONOUNS	
WH- QUESTION WORD	
What	happened then?
Which	do you prefer?
How much	does it cost?
How many	did you invite?

NOTES

- We can use the question words **What, Which, How much,** and **How many** as adjectives or pronouns.
- We can use **What** in information questions about people, things, ideas, and actions: *What professor do you have? What are they doing?*
- We use **Which** to ask about a choice from a specific group of people or things: *Which of these colors do you prefer?*
- We use **How much** and **How many** to ask about amounts or quantities.
- We use **How much** for non-count nouns.
- We use **How many** for plural count nouns.

What news does Emma give Rebecca?

Practice

12. Write *ADJ.* next to questions with **What** or **Which** as an adjective. Write *PRON.* next to questions with **What** or **Which** as a pronoun.

1. ___ADJ.___ Which room does Rebecca find Emma in?

2. ___PRON.___ What does Rebecca need to do?

3. _____ What do they talk about?

4. _____ What news does Emma give Rebecca?

5. _____ Which friend does Rebecca see next?

6. _____ Which of her professors is she going to see?

13. Write **How much** or **How many**.

1. ___How many___ players are on the team?

2. _____ money will I need?

3. _____ employees work there?

4. _____ does it cost?

5. _____ experience does he have?

6. _____ are there in your group?

14. Write questions with **Which** + noun. Ask about the underlined information.

1. I'll take the early flight. Which flight will you take?

2. He caught the 5:50 train. _____

3. I like the blue shoes. _____

4. We listen to the country music station. _____

5. He took all the photographs on the wall. _____

15. Write questions about the missing information. Use **How much** or **How many**.

1. I called . . . friends. How many friends did you call?

2. He has . . . roommates. _____

3. We need . . . sugar. _____

4. There are . . . cats in my building. _____

5. He can eat . . . _____

POWER Practice

16. PRETEND: Your friend is taking courses at a local college. Write six questions for your friend with **How much** and **How many**. Use the words in the box or words of your own.

Examples: *How many computer courses are there?*
How much homework do you have?

courses	homework	students	time	tuition	weeks

1. _____

2. _____

3. _____

4. _____

5. _____

6. _____

17. PRETEND: You are going to call a restaurant for information about the food, the hours, the location, and so on. Write three questions with **What** as an adjective (**What** + noun). Write three questions with **What** as a pronoun (**What** alone). Use your own paper.

Examples: *What kind of food do you serve? What is your specialty?*

REVIEW: PRESENT PERFECT TENSE, AFFIRMATIVE AND NEGATIVE STATEMENTS

AFFIRMATIVE STATEMENTS		
SUBJECT	HAVE/ HAS	PAST PARTICIPLE
I We You They	have	finished.
He She It	has	

NEGATIVE STATEMENTS			
SUBJECT	HAVE/ HAS	NOT	PAST PARTICIPLE
I We You They	have	not	finished.
He She It	has		

 NOTES

- Actions in the present perfect tense began in the past. Some actions and situations have ended: *She has visited New York.* But some actions and situations continue into the present: *We have lived here for a long time.* (*We still live here.*)
- We use [subject + auxiliary verb **have/has** (+ **not**) + past participle of main verb] for present perfect tense statements.
- Regular past participles are [simple form of main verb + **-ed** or **-d**].
- We can use **just** in affirmative statements about actions completed recently: *The mail has just arrived.*
- We can use **yet** in negative statements about actions or situations that haven't happened but might happen in the future: *We haven't cleaned up yet.*
- We can use **already** in affirmative statements for emphasis: *I don't have any more homework. I've already done it.*

AFFIRMATIVE CONTRACTIONS
I've, we've, you've, they've
he's, she's, it's

NEGATIVE CONTRACTIONS	
I, we, you, they	haven't
he, she, it	hasn't

Rebecca gets a hug. Ramón and Alex **have missed** her.

Practice

1. Underline the verbs in the present perfect tense.

Rebecca <u>has returned</u> to San Francisco. She has just visited Emma at the after-school program, and she has learned about losing her job. Then she sees Ramón outside. She hasn't called him since her return. He and Alex have missed her, and they both hug her. But Rebecca has to leave. She hasn't attended classes for weeks, and she needs to talk to her college advisor. She has scheduled an appointment with him.

2. Write **has** or **have**.

1. I ___have___ just telephoned.

2. The weather _____ changed.

3. You _____ asked good questions.

4. She _____ not called me yet.

5. The plane _____ not landed yet.

6. They _____ just hired a new manager.

3. Change these affirmative statements to negative statements. Use contractions.

1. He's cleaned up.

   He hasn't cleaned up.

2. She's looked everywhere.

   _____

3. You've changed.

   _____

4. It's rained a lot recently.

   _____

5. They've helped us.

   _____

6. I've cleaned my room.

   _____

4. Look at Rebecca's list of things to do. She has finished only the things marked with a check (✔). Write an affirmative statement about each thing on the list that she has done. Write a negative statement with **yet** for each thing on the list that she hasn't done. Use the present perfect tense.

```
         TO DO
  ✔ talk to Nancy
    unpack my suitcase
  ✔ call Professor Thomas
  ✔ talk to Emma
  ✔ thank Ramón and Alex
    thank Alberto
    call Kevin
    start studying
```

1. Rebecca has talked to Nancy.
2. She hasn't unpacked her suitcase yet.
3. _____
4. _____
5. _____
6. _____
7. _____
8. _____

POWER Practice

5. Write your own list of things to do. Check (✔) the things you've already finished. Write an affirmative or negative statement about each thing on your list. Use the present perfect tense.

Examples: ✔ *call Sonia*   *I've called my friend Sonia.*

wash my clothes   *I haven't washed my clothes yet.*

```
        TO DO



```

1. _____
2. _____
3. _____
4. _____
5. _____
6. _____

REVIEW: CONTRAST PRESENT PERFECT TENSE AND SIMPLE PAST TENSE

PRESENT PERFECT TENSE			
SUBJECT	*HAVE/HAS*	PAST PARTICIPLE	
We	**have**	lived	here since 1990.
She	**has**		here for ten years.

SIMPLE PAST TENSE		
SUBJECT	SIMPLE PAST TENSE FORM	
We	lived	there in 1990.
She		there for ten years.

NOTES

- We can use the present perfect tense for actions and situations that began in the past and continue into the present. We cannot use the simple past tense for these actions and situations.
- We can also use the present perfect tense for actions and situations that ended in the past. We don't say when they happened: *I've finished.*
- We can use the simple past tense for actions and situations that began and ended in the past.
- We can use [**for** + amount of time] with the present perfect or the simple past tense.
- We can use only the present perfect tense with [**since** + time/day/date/event]. These actions and situations continue into the present.

Rebecca **has** just **returned** to the college.

She **missed** a lot of classes in the weeks after her father's death.

Practice

6. Underline the verbs in the present perfect tense. Circle the verbs in the simple past tense.

Rebecca <u>has missed</u> a lot of classes. Earlier today, she (called) Professor Thomas and asked for an appointment. Rebecca has just talked with him in his office. He has discussed her situation with her other professors. Rebecca listened carefully while he explained her choices: study hard and take the exams, or repeat the semester. She has decided to take the exams. Professor Thomas wished her luck, and he handed her a sample exam.

7. Circle the correct verb.

1. He (called) / has called me last night.

2. They <u>worked / have worked</u> there since 1992.

3. I <u>decided / have decided</u> this yesterday.

4. He wants a motorcycle. He <u>wanted / has wanted</u> a motorcycle for years.

5. They <u>moved / have moved</u> to an new apartment last month.

6. I <u>loved / have loved</u> chocolate since I was a child.

7. We <u>walked / have walked</u> for an hour, and then we rested for a while.

8. Write *for* or *since*.

1. It rained ___for___ days in August.

2. We've worked _____ hours.

3. They've studied together _____ May.

4. She loved him _____ a long time.

5. They've owned it _____ 1997.

6. He watched TV _____ an hour.

7. You've helped them _____ years.

8. I've liked her _____ we were children.

9. Use the present perfect tense or the simple past tense of the verb in parentheses.

1. (seem) He ___has seemed___ quiet since his friend died.

2. (start) They ___started___ the job yesterday.

3. (wait) We _____ for an hour by now.

4. (work) They _____ there since they moved to the city.

5. (live) He _____ there since last spring.

6. (study) I _____ a lot last night.

7. (change) He _____ his mind an hour ago.

8. (talk) We _____ several times since last weekend.

9. (work) She _____ in Boston from 1993-1997.

10. (want) I _____ to talk to you ever since I heard the news.

POWER Practice

10. Complete these pairs of sentences about your life. Use the present perfect tense in the second sentence of each pair.

Example: *I live in Miami. I have lived here since 1997.*
I like basketball. I have liked basketball since I was eight.

1. I live in _____. I _____ here since _____

2. I study English. I _____ English for _____

3. I use this book. I _____ this book for _____

4. I like _____. I _____ since _____

5. I want _____. I _____ for _____

6. I listen to _____. I _____ since _____

IRREGULAR SIMPLE PAST TENSE FORMS AND PAST PARTICIPLES

SIMPLE FORM	SIMPLE PAST TENSE FORM	PAST PARTICIPLE
be	was/were	been
begin	began	begun
bring	brought	brought
catch	caught	caught
come	came	come
do	did	done
eat	ate	eaten

SIMPLE FORM	SIMPLE PAST TENSE FORM	PAST PARTICIPLE
find	found	found
give	gave	given
go	went	gone
have	had	had
hear	heard	heard
make	made	made
meet	met	met

SIMPLE FORM	SIMPLE PAST TENSE FORM	PAST PARTICIPLE
pay	paid	paid
read	read	read
say	said	said
see	saw	seen
sell	sold	sold
speak	spoke	spoken
tell	told	told

NOTES
- Regular simple past tense forms and regular past participles use [simple form of main verb + **-ed** or **-d**].
- Some verbs have irregular simple past tense forms and past participles.

In the evening, Alberto **went** to Nancy's house.

He **saw** Rebecca. He **said**, "**I've brought** something for you."

Practice

11. Check (✔) the form of the underlined verb in each sentence.

	SIMPLE FORM	SIMPLE PAST TENSE FORM	PAST PARTICIPLE
1. Rebecca has <u>seen</u> Angela and Melaku.			✔
2. Did Rebecca <u>go</u> upstairs to study?			
3. Alberto <u>came</u> to see Rebecca.			
4. He has <u>brought</u> two tickets to the opera.			
5. Does Rebecca <u>have</u> time to go to the opera?			
6. Angela <u>told</u> Rebecca to go out and have fun.			

12. Complete the sentence with the present perfect tense of the verb in parentheses.

1. (be) I ___have been___ here for an hour.

2. (make) He _____ a mistake.

3. (do) They _____ all the work.

4. (eat) We _____ there before.

5. (go) She _____ home.

6. (speak) They _____ on the phone.

7. (find) You _____ my keys.

8. (tell) I _____ the truth.

9. (see) We _____ that movie.

10. (meet) He _____ her family.

11. (hear) She _____ the news.

12. (be) You _____ a good friend.

13. Write the irregular verbs in the correct places in the chart below.

build, built, built	cut, cut, cut	hit, hit, hit	put, put, put	take, took, taken
buy, bought, bought	drive, drove, driven	hold, held, held	send, sent, sent	teach, taught, taught
cost, cost, cost	grow, grew, grown	hurt, hurt, hurt	steal, stole, stolen	write, wrote, written

The three forms are the same:				The three forms are all different:				The simple past tense form and the past participle are the same:		
SIMPLE FORM	**SIMPLE PAST TENSE FORM**	**PAST PARTICIPLE**		**SIMPLE FORM**	**SIMPLE PAST TENSE FORM**	**PAST PARTICIPLE**		**SIMPLE FORM**	**SIMPLE PAST TENSE FORM**	**PAST PARTICIPLE**
1. *cut*	*cut*	*cut*		1. *take*	*took*	*taken*		1. *send*	*sent*	*sent*
2.				2.				2.		
3.				3.				3.		
4.				4.				4.		
5.				5.				5.		

14. Complete the sentences. Use the verbs in the box. Use the present perfect tense.

build	buy	cut	drive	grow	send	teach	write

1. I ___have written___ a letter to my grandmother.

2. They _____ a new bridge.

3. We _____ the letter to him.

4. I _____ my hand with the knife.

5. She _____ a bus.

6. You _____ new shoes.

7. He _____ a moustache.

8. They _____ English for years.

POWER Practice

15. Look at the list in the box below. Which things have you done? Write affirmative and negative sentences about your experiences. Use the present perfect tense. Use your own paper.

Example: *I have given blood several times.*
I haven't bought a car.

eat octopus	pay taxes	buy a car
catch a fish	read an English newspaper	give blood

16. Now write about other experiences. Write five sentences about things you have done. Write five sentences about things you haven't done. Use the present perfect tense. Use your own paper.

Examples: *I've studied three languages.*
I haven't seen the Great Wall of China.

REVIEW: PRESENT PERFECT TENSE, YES/NO QUESTIONS AND SHORT ANSWERS

YES/NO QUESTIONS		
HAVE/HAS	SUBJECT	PAST PARTICIPLE
Have	I we you they	eaten?
Has	he she it	

SHORT ANSWERS		
YES/NO	SUBJECT	HAVE/HAS (+ NOT)
Yes,	we	have.
	she	has.
No,	we	have not. haven't.
	she	has not. hasn't.

NOTES

- We use [auxiliary verb **Have/Has** + subject + past participle of main verb] for **Yes/No** questions in the present perfect tense.
- We can use **ever** in **Yes/No** questions to mean *at any time in the past: Have you ever been to Australia?*
- We can use **yet** in **Yes/No** questions to ask about actions or situations we expect to happen: *Have you done your homework yet?*
- We use [subject + **have/has**] for short answers with **Yes**.
- We use [subject + **have/has** + **not**] for short answers with **No**.

Bill: *Have* you *ever heard* of the Moles?

Rebecca: Yes, I *have*. They're a hard rock group, aren't they?

Practice

1. Check (✔) the **Yes/No** questions in the present perfect tense.

1. __✔__ Has Rebecca been in the library?

2. _____ Has she finished studying?

3. _____ Is she confident about her exams?

4. _____ Has Bill helped her?

5. _____ Does Bill have an audition?

6. _____ Have they agreed to go together?

2. Put the words in order. Write **Yes/No** questions.

1. done / this / has / before / he / ever   _Has he ever done this before?_

2. you / visited / ever / have / Disney World   _____

3. made / a / I / mistake / have   _____

4. bought / has / she / car / new / a   _____

5. ever / written / you / a / have / poem   _____

6. he / eaten / lobster / ever / has   _____

7. have / listened / you / this / tape / to   _____

3. Change the statements to *Yes/No* questions. Write short answers.

1. I haven't seen them. <u>Have you seen them? No, I haven't.</u>

2. They haven't finished. _____

3. She's gone home. _____

4. We've eaten. _____

5. It hasn't begun. _____

4. Complete the *Yes/No* questions about the story. Use the present perfect tense of the verb in parentheses.

1. Rebecca / (be) <u>Has Rebecca been</u> _____ busy with her studies?

2. she / (go) _____ to the library every day this week?

3. Bill / (help) _____ Rebecca with her studies?

4. he / (be) _____ happy at school this semester?

5. he / (make) _____ plans for an audition?

6. Rebecca / (promise) _____ to go to the audition?

POWER Practice

5. Write short answers to these *Yes/No* questions about your past experiences.

Examples: *Have you ever seen a rainbow?*   *Yes, I have. (or) No, I haven't.*

1. Have you ever climbed a mountain? _____

2. Have you ever found something valuable? _____

3. Have you ever spoken to a famous person? _____

4. Have you ever held a baby? _____

5. Have you ever taught a class? _____

6. Have you ever been in a car accident? _____

6. Write six *Yes/No* questions for a friend. Ask about past experiences. Use the present perfect tense + *ever*. Use your own paper.

Examples: *Have you ever bought a lottery ticket?*
Have you ever been to an art museum?

REVIEW: PRESENT PERFECT TENSE, *WH-* QUESTIONS

WH- QUESTION WORD (+ NOUN)	HAVE/ HAS	SUBJECT	PAST PARTICIPLE
Who Whom	has	he	invited?
What	have	you	bought?
When	has	it	failed?
Where	has	she	been?
How long	have	I	studied?
How much (fruit) How many (hats)	have	we	sold?
Which sports	have	you	played?
What cities	has	he	seen?

WHO/WHAT AS SUBJECT	HAS	PAST PARTICIPLE
Who	has	finished?
What		happened?

NOTES

- We can use [Wh- question word or phrase + auxiliary verb **have/has** + subject + past participle of main verb] for information questions in the present perfect tense.
- We use [**Who/What** + auxiliary verb **has** + past participle of main verb] for information questions about the subject.
- We use [**Who/Whom/What** + auxiliary verb **have/has** + subject + past participle of main verb] in questions about the object.
- The phrase **How long** in present perfect tense questions asks how much time has passed from the beginning of an action or a situation to the present moment.

Alberto: **What have** you **decided** about the opera?

Practice

7. Check (✔) the *Wh-* questions in the present perfect tense.

1. ✔ What has Rebecca decided?

2. _____ Who goes to the opera alone?

3. _____ When does Alberto go to see Ramón?

4. _____ Where has Alberto been?

5. _____ What has Alberto decided to do?

6. _____ How long have he and Rebecca known each other?

8. Write *Who, Whom, What, When, Where, How long, How much,* or *How many*.

1. Whom _____ have they invited to dinner? Several business associates.

2. _____ has he done? He's written many books.

3. _____ have you been? At the movies.

4. _____ has heard the news? Almost everyone.

5. _____ have they been here? For about an hour.

6. _____ have you gone fishing? Every summer since I was little.

7. _____ money have you spent? About $100.

8. _____ courses has she taken? Five.

9. Write *Wh-* questions. Use the present perfect tense of the verb in parentheses.

1. who / (arrive)   Who has arrived?

2. what / they / (do)   What have they done?

3. what / (happen)   _____

4. how long / you / (know) / the truth   _____

5. which foot / he / (hurt)   _____

6. what kind of car / she / (buy)   _____

7. how much rain / we / (have)   _____

10. Write *Wh-* questions about the <u>underlined</u> information. Use *Who, What, How much*, and *How long*.

1. <u>My brother</u> has graduated.   Who has graduated?

2. They have decided <u>to buy it</u>.   What have they decided?

3. <u>An accident</u> has happened.   _____

4. I've known her <u>for ten years</u>.   _____

5. They've had <u>a foot of</u> snow.   _____

6. We've been home <u>since 6:00 p.m.</u>   _____

7. They've asked <u>the President</u>.   _____

POWER Practice

11. Write your answers. Use *for* or *since*.

Example: How long have you lived in your home?   For many years. (or) Since 1980.

1. How long have you lived in your home?   _____

2. How long have you studied English?   _____

3. How long have you wanted to learn English?   _____

4. How long have you had this book?   _____

5. How long have you worked on this exercise?   _____

12. Write eight *Wh-* questions for a friend. Use the present perfect tense. Use your own paper.

Examples: How long have you lived here?   How many English courses have you taken?

REFLEXIVE PRONOUNS

	SUBJECT	VERB	REFLEXIVE PRONOUN	
S I N G U L A R	I		myself	
	You		yourself	
	He		himself	
	She	hurt	herself	in the accident.
	It		itself	
P L U R A L	We		ourselves	
	You		yourselves	
	They		themselves	

	BY	REFLEXIVE PRONOUN
I did it	**by**	myself.
They prefer to study		themselves.

 NOTES

- We use reflexive pronouns when the subject and the object refer to the same person or thing: *She bought herself a present.*
- We use [**by** + reflexive pronoun] to mean *alone*: *She walks to school by herself.*
- Singular reflexive pronouns end in **-self**, and plural reflexive pronouns end in **-selves**. There is a singular *and* a plural reflexive form for **you**: *yourself, yourselves.*

Alberto talks with his brother. He's feeling sorry for ***himself***.

Practice

13. Circle the reflexive pronouns.

Alberto is feeling sorry for (himself.) Rebecca doesn't want to see him right now. She needs to be by herself to study. She wouldn't go to the opera with him, so Alberto went by himself. Now he's telling his troubles to Ramón. They're in the restaurant by themselves. Ramón tells Alberto, "Stop thinking about yourself. Rebecca needs some understanding right now. Be patient." Alberto responds, "Me . . . patient? I've never been patient in my entire life." He knows himself well.

14. Fill in the blanks with reflexive pronouns.

1. Rebecca: *I need to be by* _____myself_____ .

2. Alberto: *Rebecca, take care of* _____. *Don't work too hard.*

3. Alberto: *She needs time by* _____.

4. Mrs. Mendoza: *Ramón, Alberto—will you be by* _____ *for Christmas?*

5. Ramón: *Mama, I promise—we'll take care of* _____.

6. Rebecca: *Dad didn't take care of* _____.

15. Write the sentences. Use the simple past tense. Add *by* + a reflexive pronoun.

1. they / (build) / the house   They built the house by themselves.

2. he / (live)   _____

3. the girl / (do) / it   _____

4. we / (want) / to be   _____

5. I / (come) / here   _____

16. Complete the sentences. Use words from the box. Add a reflexive pronoun.

angry at	dress	help	interested in	pleased with	proud of	wash

1. I'm very _pleased with myself_____ because I finished everything on time.

2. A cat will _____ with its tongue.

3. Both of you got excellent grades. You should be _____

4. They're _____ because they got terrible grades.

5. The little boy can _____, but he can't tie his shoes yet.

6. She is very self-centered. She is only_____.

7. Nobody else can help us. We have to _____.

POWER Practice

17. Write six *Yes/No* questions for a friend. What has he/she has done alone? Use the present perfect tense + *by yourself*. Use your own paper.

Example: *Have you ever lived by yourself?*

18. Write six statements about things you do by yourself. Use your own paper.

Examples: *I usually study by myself.*
              I go to the supermarket by myself.

PAST PERFECT TENSE, AFFIRMATIVE AND NEGATIVE STATEMENTS

AFFIRMATIVE STATEMENTS			NEGATIVE STATEMENTS				AFFIRMATIVE CONTRACTIONS	NEGATIVE CONTRACTIONS		NOTES
SUBJECT	HAD	PAST PARTICIPLE	SUBJECT	HAD	NOT	PAST PARTICIPLE	[SUBJECT + HAD]	SUBJECT	[HAD + NOT]	
I We You They He She It	had	eaten.	I We You They He She It	had	not	eaten.	I'd we'd you'd they'd he'd she'd It'd	I we you they he she it	hadn't	• We use the past perfect tense for one action or situation in the past before another action, situation, or time in the past: *He had done his homework before he played tennis. He had finished it by 4:00.* • We use [subject + auxiliary verb **had** (+ **not**) + past participle] for past perfect tense statements. • We can use the same adverbs with the past perfect tense and with the present perfect tense: **just**, **already**, **yet**, **ever**, and **never**. We can also use the same time expressions with **for** and **since**.

Mr. Wang wanted to talk to his wife. He **had just received** an important letter. She **hadn't read** the letter **yet**.

Practice

1. Underline the verbs in the past perfect tense.

Ramón took Alex to the airport, and he said good-bye. He <u>had agreed</u> to send Alex to L.A. for Christmas. Next, Ramón delivered Alex's present to Vincent. He had promised to do that. After Ramón had gone, Mr. Wang came home. He wanted to talk to his wife because he had received an important letter. A company in Taiwan had offered him a job, and he wanted to move there. The news upset Mrs. Wang. She hadn't expected it.

2. Rewrite the sentences using contractions.

1. I had seen the movie before.　　　　　　*I'd seen the movie before.*

2. They had never called me.

3. He had won the race.

4. It had not begun to rain.

5. We had waited a long time.

3. Use the verbs in parentheses to complete the sentences about the story. Use the past perfect tense.

Ramón was unhappy. He (be, never) _had never been_ away from his son for Christmas before. He (agree) _____ to put Alex on a plane to L.A., but he didn't want to do it. Alex wasn't happy, either. He (promise) _____ to spend Christmas with his mother, but he wanted to stay home. His friend Vincent was unhappy, too. He (hear) _____ the conversation between his parents about the move to Taiwan. This plan surprised Vincent. He (not, expect) _____ it.

4. Explain each situation. Write negative statements in the past perfect tense. Use the verbs in parentheses.

1. The man looked tired. (sleep)   _He hadn't slept well._

2. My room was messy. (clean)   _____

3. I was very hungry. (eat)   _____

4. My friends were at home. (go)   _____

5. The streets were dry. (rain)   _____

6. My homework was only half done. (finish)   _____

5. Explain each situation. Write an affirmative statement or a negative statement. Use the past perfect tense.

1. The movie theater was empty.   _Everybody had left._

2. The floor was wet.   _____

3. The little boy was crying.   _____

4. The woman arrived late for work.   _____

5. The refrigerator was empty.   _____

6. The man had a black eye.   _____

POWER Practice

6. Write six statements about things you did for the first time. Tell when you did each thing. Use the simple past tense. Write a second statement in the past perfect tense with **never** and **before**. Use your own paper.

Examples: *I bought a car in 1991. I had never owned a car before.*
I ate a papaya yesterday. I had never tasted a papaya before.

PAST PERFECT TENSE AND SIMPLE PAST TENSE

1st ACTION/SITUATION			2nd ACTION/SITUATION		
	SUBJECT	PAST PERFECT TENSE VERB		SUBJECT	SIMPLE PAST TENSE VERB
	We	had finished	before by the time when	they	arrived.
After As soon as	we	had finished,			

2nd ACTION/SITUATION			1st ACTION/SITUATION		
	SUBJECT	SIMPLE PAST TENSE VERB		SUBJECT	PAST PERFECT TENSE VERB
	They	arrived	after as soon as	we	had finished.
Before By the time When	they	arrived,			

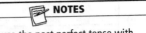

NOTES

- We use the past perfect tense with the simple past tense to show the order of two actions or situations in the past.
- We use the past perfect tense for the action or situation that happened first.
- We use the simple past tense for the second action.
- We can also use [simple past + simple past] to show two past actions or situations when we use **before** or **after:** *I finished before they arrived. After they arrived, we had dinner.*

When Ramón **went** to see Rebecca, he **had** already **taken** Alex to the airport.

Practice

7. Check (✔) the statements with both a simple past tense verb and a past perfect tense verb. Underline the simple past tense verbs. Circle the past perfect tense verbs.

1. ✔ Ramón <u>went</u> to deliver Rebecca's present after he (had given) his promise to Alex.

2. _____ Before he went there, he had already delivered Vincent's present to the Wangs' house.

3. _____ After Rebecca had invited Ramón in, they talked for a while.

4. _____ Ramón didn't leave immediately after he gave Rebecca her present.

5. _____ Both Rebecca and Ramón expected to be alone for Christmas.

6. _____ Ramón felt like a fool as soon as he had asked Rebecca to spend Christmas with him.

8. Write *1* next to the action Rosa did first. Underline the verb in that clause.

1. _____ Before Rosa got into the shower, __1__ she <u>had turned on</u> the coffee maker.

2. _____ After she had washed her hair, _____ she drank her coffee.

3. _____ She got dressed _____ as soon as she had dried her hair.

4. _____ She had finished dressing _____ when the phone rang.

9. Complete each sentence. Use the verb in parentheses. Use the simple past tense.

1. (arrive) By the time he _____arrived_____ at the airport, the plane had left.

2. (go) By the time she _____ on vacation, she'd finished all her work.

3. (finish) He'd already won the election before we _____ counting the votes.

4. (give) The boss _____ me a raise after I'd received several other job offers.

5. (be) All the students had finished the test by the time the class _____ over.

6. (decide) He _____ to buy the car only after he'd driven it several times.

10. Complete each sentence. Use the verb in parentheses. Use the past perfect tense.

1. (leave) By the time I got to the station, my train _____had left_____.

2. (wash) They came into the kitchen in muddy shoes after I _____ just _____ the floor.

3. (make) Before they went to the restaurant, they _____ a reservation.

4. (hear) We _____ good reports of the movie before we went to see it.

5. (meet) By the time he called her for a date, she _____ someone else.

6 (fail) The student went to a tutor for help after he _____ a test.

POWER Practice

11. Complete the sentences about yourself. Use the past perfect tense.

Example: *By the time I left, I had been at the mall for hours.*

My family had already eaten dinner by the time I got home.

1. By the time I left, _____.

2. After I _____, I had some breakfast.

3. _____ by the time I got home.

4. _____ before I went to bed last night.

5. Before I started this exercise, _____.

12. Think about times you were late for something. Write five sentences about things that had already happened in your absence. Use *By the time I* + the simple past tense in the first clause. Use the past perfect tense in the second clause for the action that had already happened. Use your own paper.

Examples: *By the time I got to school, the teacher had already taken attendance.*

By the time I arrived at the game, it had started.

PAST PERFECT TENSE: *YES/NO* QUESTIONS AND SHORT ANSWERS

YES/NO QUESTIONS		
HAD	SUBJECT	PAST PASTICIPLE
Had	I we you they he she it	eaten?

SHORT ANSWERS		
YES/NO	SUBJECT	HAD (+ NOT)
Yes,	I we you they he she it	had.
No,		had not. hadn't.

NOTES

- We use [auxiliary verb **Had** + subject + past participle] in **Yes/No** questions in the past perfect tense.
- We can use **ever** in **Yes/No** questions to mean *at any earlier time: Had the store manager ever seen the robber before?*
- We use [subject + **had**] for short answers with **Yes** in the past perfect tense.
- We use [subject + **had** + **not**] for short answers with **No** in the past perfect tense.

Had Alberto **expected** the visit from Ramón?
No, he **hadn't**. It came as a surprise.

Practice

13. Check (✔) the *Yes/No* questions in the past perfect tense.

1. ✔ Before this visit, had Ramón ever been to Alberto's office before?

2. _____ Had Alberto expected to see his brother this afternoon?

3. _____ Had Alberto already made plans for his ski trip?

4. _____ Did the two brothers talk about Rebecca?

5. _____ Did Alberto understand Ramón's feelings for Rebecca?

6. _____ Had Alberto ever noticed Ramón's feelings for her before?

14. Last month Ayako saw her family in Japan for the first time after a year in the United States. Write *Yes/No* questions for her about her visit home. Use the past perfect tense.

1. your family / change   Had your family changed?

2. your parents / grow / older   _____

3. your little sister / miss / you _____

4. your little brother / grow / taller _____

5. your friends / change   _____

6. your neighborhood / stay / the same _____

15. Change statements 1-6 to *Yes/No* questions. Write short answers.

I promised to meet my friends at the movie theater, but I was late. (1) My friends had already gone inside. (2) The movie had already begun. (3) They hadn't sold all the tickets. (4) My friends had saved a seat for me. (5) We hadn't seen this film before. (6) I hadn't missed much of it.

1. Had your friends already gone inside? Yes, they had._____

2. _____

3. _____

4. _____

5. _____

6. _____

16. Write a *Yes/No* question about each statement. Use the past perfect tense + *ever* and *before*.

1. I went skiing.   Had you ever gone skiing before?_____

2. He visited Disney World.   _____

3. She met his parents.   _____

4. We danced the tango.   _____

5. They bought a car.   _____

POWER Practice

17. Write short conversations. You report a new experience using the simple past tense. Then the second person asks a *Yes/No* question using the past perfect tense + *before*. Use your own paper.

Example: *You: Doctor, I had a terrible headache.*
   Doctor: Had you ever had a headache like that before?
   You: No, I hadn't.

1. You are talking to your doctor. You sprained your ankle.

2. Your are talking to a neighbor. You gave blood at the hospital.

3. You are talking to a friend. You went to _____.

18. PRETEND: You are talking to someone else who is watching *Connect with English* and using this book. Write four *Yes/No* questions for this person about his/her experiences learning English in the past. Use the past perfect tense. Use your own paper.

Examples: *Before you started* Connect with English, *had you studied English?*
   Had you ever seen a video like this before?

THE AUDITION

WH- QUESTIONS WITH *HOW OFTEN*; FREQUENCY EXPRESSIONS; ADVERBS OF FREQUENCY

WH- QUESTIONS WITH *HOW OFTEN*				
HOW OFTEN	**AUX.**	**SUBJECT**	**MAIN VERB**	
How often	do	they		there?
	did	he	go	downtown?
	can	she		on vacation?
	have	you	walked	to school?
	BE AS MAIN VERB	**SUBJECT**		
	is	it	late?	
	were	they	here?	

ANSWERS
FREQUENCY EXPRESSIONS
Once a week.
He went **twice a month**.
Three times a year.
We walk **every day**.
Once in a while.
Every summer.

NOTES

- We use **Wh-** questions with **How often** to ask about the frequency of a situation.
- Frequency expressions and adverbs of frequency tell how often a situation happens.
- We usually put an adverb of frequency *before* the main verb.
- We put an adverb of frequency *after* **BE** (+ **not**) in the simple present or simple past tense: *She is always here.*
- We can use **sometimes**, **usually**, and **frequently** at the beginning or the end of a sentence: *Sometimes I feel lonely. I feel lonely sometimes.*

ADVERBS OF FREQUENCY	PERCENT OF TIME
always	100%
usually	↑
often/frequently	
sometimes	
rarely	
never	0%

ADVERBS OF FREQUENCY IN STATEMENTS			
SUBJECT	**(AUX.)**	**ADVERB**	**MAIN VERB**
We		always	win.
They	don't	usually	complain.
It		often	happened.
She	has	never	skied.
SUBJECT	**BE AS MAIN VERB (+NOT)**	**ADVERB**	
He	is	rarely	late.
She	wasn't	often	home.

How often does Rebecca drink coffee?
Every day. She **usually** drinks it black, but tonight she wants sugar.

Practice

1. Underline the adverbs of frequency and the frequency expressions. Circle the verbs.

1. Rebecca often (talks) with Nancy.

2. She (sees) Nancy every day.

3. Nancy is always interested in Rebecca's life.

4. Once in a while Nancy asks Rebecca personal questions.

5. Rebecca usually answers Nancy's questions.

6. Sometimes Rebecca doesn't want to talk about her feelings.

2. Match the *Wh-* questions and answers. Write the letters.

1. __b__ How often do buses stop here?
2. _____ When do people celebrate Christmas?
3. _____ How often do you pay your bills?
4. _____ How long was your conversation?

a. Once a month.
✔b. Every 20 minutes.
c. On December 25.
d. Ten minutes.

3. Write questions with *How often* to match the answers.

1. How often do you see him? _____ I see him once a week.
2. _____ She went there every weekend.
3. _____ They pay me twice a month.
4. _____ I visit them once in a while.

4. Rewrite each sentence with the adverb of frequency in parentheses.

1. (rarely) They are here on time.   They are rarely here on time.
2. (always) She doesn't do a good job.   _____
3. (never) He eats junk food.   _____
4. (often) You call her.   _____
5. (always) I am happy to see you.   _____

POWER Practice

5. Answer questions about yourself.

Examples: How often do you drink coffee? I never drink coffee. How often do you shop? Once a week.

1. How often do you go to a concert?   _____
2. How often do you go to the supermarket?   _____
3. How often do you practice speaking English? _____
4. How often do you go to the movies?   _____

6. Write six sentences about your everyday life. Use adverbs of frequency or frequency expressions. Use your own paper.

Examples: I always do my homework. I eat breakfast once in a while.

WH- QUESTIONS WITH HOW AND ADVERBS OF MANNER

WH- QUESTIONS WITH HOW					ANSWERS
HOW	AUX.	SUBJECT	MAIN VERB		ADVERBS OF MANNER
How	does	he	drive?		Fast.
	did	they	do	the work?	Carefully.
	has	she	performed	so far?	Well.
	were	you	playing	the music?	Quietly.

 NOTES

- We can use **How** in **Wh-** questions to ask about the way an action happens.
- We can use adverbs of manner to answer these questions with **How.** An adverb of manner describes the action of a verb.
- We can often use [adjective + **-ly**] to form an adverb of manner.
- We put an adverb of manner at the end of a clause: *He always works hard. You can improve your English slowly.*

Rebecca: *I don't want to wait. Let's go!*

How does Rebecca speak to Bill? **Impatiently**.

Practice

7. Underline the verbs. Circle the adverbs of manner.

1. Rebecca and Bill wait (quietly) for their audition.

2. They spoke politely to the manager.

3. Bill can play the guitar very well.

4. Rebecca can sing beautifully.

5. Rebecca has studied very hard for her exams.

6. She writes fast when she takes an exam.

8. Put the words in order. Write **Wh-** questions with **How.**

1. does / she / piano / how / play / the   How does she play the piano?

2. was / team / the / playing / how   _____

3. has / how / new / your / car / performed   _____

4. did / you / test / on / how / the / do   _____

5. do / how / snow / in / drive / you / the   _____

6. you / sing / how / do   _____

7. was / she / how / skating   _____

8. did / talk / how / to / him / she   _____

9. Write the adjective/adverb pairs in the correct places in the charts below.

angry / angrily	easy / easily	good / well	hard / hard	quick / quickly
brave / bravely	fast / fast	happy / happily	neat / neatly	quiet / quietly

The adjective and the adverb are the same:		Adjective + -ly = adverb:		Adjective – -y +-ily = adverb:		The adverb is irregular:	
ADJ.	**ADV.**	**ADJ.**	**ADV.**	**ADJ.**	**ADV.**	**ADJ.**	**ADV.**
1. *fast*	fast	1. *brave*	*bravely*	1.		1.	
2.		2.		2.			
		3.		3.			
		4.					

10. Rewrite the sentences. Change the adjectives to adverbs with **–ly**.

1. He's a wonderful singer.   He sings wonderfully. _____

2. She's a careful driver.   _____

3. You're a quick worker.   _____

4. He's a slow reader.   _____

5. They're graceful skaters.   _____

6. I'm a bad dancer.   _____

POWER Practice

11. Answer these questions about you.

Example: How do you sing? I don't sing well.

1. How do you sing?   _____

2. Do you drive fast?   _____

3. Can you dance well?   _____

4. How do you speak English?   _____

5. How do you speak your first language?   _____

12. PRETEND: You have a new teacher. Your friend has already had this teacher. Write six questions for your friend about this teacher. Write **Yes/No** questions with adverbs of manner or **Wh-** questions with **How**. Use your own paper.

Examples: Does he mark papers clearly? How does he explain things?

WH- QUESTIONS WITH WHOSE; POSSESSIVE ADJECTIVES, NOUNS, AND PRONOUNS

WH- QUESTIONS WITH WHOSE				ANSWERS
WHOSE (+ NOUN)	**AUX.**	**SUBJECT**	**MAIN VERB**	
Whose car	did	he	drive?	**My car.**
Whose pen	are	you	using?	**The teacher's.**
Whose	can	I	borrow?	**Mine.**
WHOSE (+ NOUN)	**BE AS MAIN VERB**	**SUBJECT**		
Whose girlfriend	is	that?		**John's.**
Whose	were	those?		**Ours.**

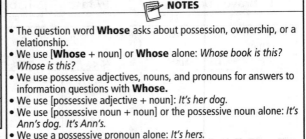

NOTES

- The question word **Whose** asks about possession, ownership, or a relationship.
- We use [**Whose** + noun] or **Whose** alone: *Whose book is this? Whose is this?*
- We use possessive adjectives, nouns, and pronouns for answers to information questions with **Whose.**
- We use [possessive adjective + noun]: *It's her dog.*
- We use [possessive noun + noun] or the possessive noun alone: *It's Ann's dog. It's Ann's.*
- We use a possessive pronoun alone: *It's hers.*

R	SUBJECT PRONOUNS	POSSESSIVE ADJECTIVES	POSSESSIVE PRONOUNS	POSSESSIVE NOUNS
E	I	my	mine	
V	we	our	ours	
	you	your	yours	
I	they	their	theirs	the Caseys'
E	he	his	his	the man's
	she	her	hers	Rebecca's
W	it	its	its	the dog's

Whose song is Rebecca singing?

It's **hers**.

Practice

13. Match the **Wh-** questions and answers. Write the letters.

1. __c__ Whose friend is Bill?

2. _____ How often have they auditioned together?

3. _____ Whose idea was the audition?

4. _____ Whose song does Rebecca sing?

5. _____ How does she sing?

a. This is the first time.

b. Beautifully.

✔**c.** Rebecca's.

d. It was Bill's.

e. Her song.

14. Circle the correct possessive word.

1. That's (my) / mine book.

2. This book is Ann's / her.

3. That's our / ours car.

4. Is this pen your / yours?

5. Their / Theirs papers are here.

6. Those boots are my / mine.

15. Put the words in order. Write **Wh-** questions with **Whose**.

1. cat / is / whose / that   Whose cat is that? _____

2. picture / whose / this / is   _____

3. you / borrow / whose / books / did   _____

4. radio / playing / is / whose   _____

5. are / whose / those   _____

16. Write questions with **Whose** about the <u>underlined</u> information.

1. She wore <u>her sister's</u> earrings.   Whose earrings did she wear? _____

2. He painted <u>his brother's</u> house.   _____

3. That is <u>Professor Smith's</u> class.   _____

4. Those are <u>my</u> papers.   _____

5. I'm using <u>my friend's</u> tennis racquet.   _____

6. We can take <u>my parents</u> car.   _____

17. Rewrite each sentence in two ways. Use possessive nouns and pronouns.

1. The car belongs to my parents.   It's my parents' car. It's theirs. _____

2. The dog belongs to Mike.   _____

3. The books belong to Jane.   _____

4. The ball belongs to my brother.   _____

5. The CDs belong to my friends.   _____

POWER Practice

18. PRETEND: Your friend's family has just celebrated Christmas. You can see many unwrapped gifts under their Christmas tree. Write five questions with **Whose** about these things. Use your own paper.

Examples: Whose shirt is that? Whose are those?

19. Write ten sentences about nice things that belong to you, your family, or your friends. Use possessive adjectives, nouns, and pronouns in your sentences. Use your own paper.

Examples: My friend Joe has a nice car. It's his.
My sister's wedding dress is very beautiful.

ADJECTIVE CLAUSES: DESCRIBING PEOPLE

INDEPENDENT CLAUSE			INDEPENDENT CLAUSE	
SUBJECT	VERB	OBJECT	SUBJECT	VERB
She	saw	the person.	The person	was swimming.

INDEPENDENT CLAUSE			ADJECTIVE CLAUSE	
SUBJECT	VERB	OBJECT	SUBJECT	VERB
She	saw	**the person**	who that	**was swimming**.

NOTES

- An independent clause includes [subject + verb]. It can function as a complete sentence.
- We can combine two independent clauses into one sentence with [independent clause + adjective clause]: *Do you know the girl who won the race?*
- An adjective clause comes *after* the noun or pronoun it describes.
- We can use either **who** or **that** as the subject in adjective clauses about people.

Rebecca and Bill talk to the man **who taped their songs**.

Practice

1. Underline the adjective clauses.

Rebecca and Bill went to audition for the Moles. Bill was the person who arranged the audition. They talked to the man who manages the Moles, but they didn't talk to the musicians who make up the band. Rebecca and Bill recorded their songs. They got copies of the tapes from the man who made them. He didn't comment on Rebecca's song, "Dreamcatcher." Bill was the one who said, "Rebecca, that was a beautiful song."

2. Match the independent clauses and their adjective clauses to complete the definitions. Write the letters.

1. __C__ An optimist is a person
2. _____ A pessimist is a person
3. _____ A fan is someone
4. _____ A workaholic is a person
5. _____ A volunteer is someone

a. that admires or supports a team or a performer.
b. who wants to work all the time.
✔**c.** who believes good things will happen.
d. who offers to do something for free.
e. that expects bad luck and trouble to come.

3. Complete the definitions. Use adjective clauses.

1. A student is _a person who is learning._

2. A musician is _____

3. An architect is _____

4. A dentist is _____

5. A coach is _____

4. Combine the two sentences into one sentence with an adjective clause. The adjective clause will describe the **boldfaced** word.

1. I met the **professor**.
   He teaches that course. _I met the professor who teaches that course._

2. I thanked the **man**.
   The man brought the mail. _____

3. We saw the **woman**.
   She had won the race. _____

4. Do you know the **people**?
   The people live in that house. _____

5. She doesn't like the **boy**.
   He sits next to her in class. _____

POWER Practice

5. Write definitions for five different types of workers. Use an adjective clause in each definition. Use your own paper.

Examples: *A pilot is a person who flies planes.*
A gas station attendant is a person who puts gas in people's cars.

6. Complete the sentences with your own definitions. Use adjective clauses.

Example: *A friend is someone who will never lie to you.*

1. A friend is _____

2. A good teacher is _____

3. A great leader is _____

4. A true hero is _____

5. A good parent is _____

ADJECTIVE CLAUSES: DESCRIBING THINGS

INDEPENDENT CLAUSE			INDEPENDENT CLAUSE	
SUBJECT	VERB	OBJECT	SUBJECT	VERB
I	bought	a camera.	The camera	doesn't work.

INDEPENDENT CLAUSE			ADJECTIVE CLAUSE	
SUBJECT	VERB	OBJECT	SUBJECT	VERB
I	bought	**a camera**	**which that**	**doesn't work**.

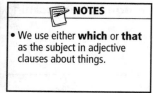

NOTES

• We use either **which** or **that** as the subject in adjective clauses about things.

Nancy has some candy **that was probably a Christmas present**.

Practice

7. Check (✔) the sentences with adjective clauses.

1. ✔ Rebecca comes home from an audition that didn't go very well.

2. _____ Nancy is sitting by the Christmas tree.

3. _____ She offers Rebecca some chocolates which look delicious.

4. _____ She tells Rebecca about the call that came from Alberto.

5. _____ Rebecca thinks about calling him back.

6. _____ Nancy offers Rebecca some advice which is about Alberto and Ramón.

8. Underline the object of the independent clause. Circle the adjective clause that describes it.

1. He bought a car that came from Germany.

2. She grows flowers that are four feet tall.

3. They have a truck which is twenty years old.

4. I read the book which won that prize.

5. Do you like chocolates that have chewy centers?

6. He wore the sweater that was a gift from his girlfriend.

7. She bought a computer that is really great.

8. Did you hear the song which the rock group sang?

9. Match the independent clauses and their adjective clauses to complete the definitions. Write the letters.

1. __c__ A knife is
2. _____ A stopwatch is
3. _____ A driver's license is
4. _____ A tape measure is
5. _____ An ID is
6. _____ A thermometer is

a. a tool that measures the length of something.
b. a permit that gives a person the right to drive.
✔**c.** a tool that can cut things.
d. an instrument which measures temperature.
e. a small clock that can time people in a race.
f. a card which has a person's name and picture.

10. Combine the two sentences into one sentence with an adjective clause. The adjective clause will describe the boldfaced word.

1. Do you have **a dictionary**?
   The dictionary is for children. _Do you have a dictionary that is for children?_
2. They have **an apartment**.
   The apartment has three bedrooms. _____
3. She likes **books**.
   The books are about love and romance. _____
4. He has a **truck**.
   The truck uses a lot of gas. _____
5. We need a **car**.
   The car gets good gas mileage. _____

POWER Practice

11. What kinds of things do you like? Describe them. Use adjective clauses.

Example: *I like movies that take place at some time back in history.*

1. I like books _____
2. I like clothes _____
3. I like cars _____
4. I like food _____

12. Where are you living? Write five sentences about your dorm, house, or apartment. Use adjective clauses. Use your own paper.

Example: *I'm living in a dorm which has four floors. I have a room that is nice and sunny.*

ADJECTIVE CLAUSES: DESCRIBING PEOPLE AND THINGS

	INDEPENDENT CLAUSE			ADJECTIVE CLAUSE		
	SUBJECT	**VERB**	**OBJECT**	**SUBJECT**	**VERB**	
PEOPLE	I	met	**some people**	who	live	**near you.**
	We	know	**someone**	that	knows	**a lot about computers.**
THINGS	I	like	**stories**	which	are	**about real events.**
	They	have	**a car**	that	doesn't run	**very well.**

NOTES

- We use **who** or **that** as the subject in adjective clauses about people.
- We use **which** or **that** as the subject in adjective clauses about things.

Rebecca wants something **that is different from Bill's idea of success**.

Practice

13. Write **P** next to sentences with adjective clauses that describe **people**. Write **T** next to sentences with adjective clauses which describe **things.**

1. __P__ Bill is a friend who knows Rebecca from school.

2. __T__ He talks about the things that matter to her.

3. _____ He describes Rebecca as a person who is very serious, maybe too serious.

4. _____ Rebecca has a voice which shows real talent.

5. _____ A career in music is something that requires more than talent.

6. _____ Bill and Rebecca have dreams that are similar in some ways but different in others.

7. _____ They are friends who enjoy making music together.

14. Circle **who** or **which**.

1. I have a friend (who) / which works for that company.

2. He wrote a letter who / which explained the problem.

3. I know someone who / which is getting married.

4. We have a car who / which needs some repairs.

5. Let's buy a picture who / which will look good on that wall.

6. They don't know anyone who / which can help them.

15. Combine the two sentences into one sentence with an adjective clause. The adjective clause will describe the **boldfaced** word.

1. We like the **teacher**.

   She teaches our son.   _We like the teacher who teaches our son._

2. He has a **guitar**.

   It belonged to his grandfather. _____

3. Do you know the **people**?

   They live next door. _____

4. She works for a **company**.

   The company makes auto parts. _____

5. I know **somebody**.

   That person writes music. _____

6. We went to a great **restaurant**.

   The restaurant serves Mexican food. _____

7. Have they hired **somebody**?

   That person knows computers. _____

8. Did you see the **accident**?

   It happened at the corner. _____

POWER Practice

16. Write your answers to the questions. Use adjective clauses.

Example: *I like people who have a sense of humor.*

1. What kind of people do you like? _____

2. What kind of people do you respect? _____

3. What kind of teachers do you like? _____

4. What kind of friends do you want? _____

5. What kind of leaders do you admire? _____

17. What things would you like to have? Write six sentences about these things. Use adjective clauses. Use your own paper.

Examples: *I'd like a house that sits on a hill by the ocean.*
I'd like some black leather boots that have three-inch heels.

REVIEW: DIRECT SPEECH

	SUBJECT	VERB	DIRECT SPEECH
FORM 1	I,	**said,**	"We're leaving."
	We, You, They,	**asked,**	"Where are you going?"
	He, She	**answered,**	"To a movie. We'll be back at 9:00."

	DIRECT SPEECH	SUBJECT	VERB
FORM 2	"We're leaving,"	I,	**said.**
	"Where are you going?"	we, you, they,	**asked.**
	"To a movie. We'll be back at 9:00,"	he, she	**answered.**

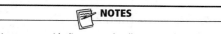 **NOTES**

- A sentence with direct speech tells a person's exact words.
- We use quotation marks (" ") before and after the person's exact words.
- A sentence with direct speech usually has a verb like **say**, **ask**, or **answer** before or after the direct speech.
- We put a comma (,) after the verb **say**, **ask**, or **answer** in Form 1 sentences.
- We put a period (.) or a question mark (?) before the final quotation marks in Form 1 sentences.
- We put a comma (,) or a question mark (?) before the final quotation marks in Form 2 sentences.

Alberto **said,** "I wanted you to have this."
"It's a beautiful photo," **said** Rebecca.

Practice

1. Underline the direct speech in each sentence.

1. Rebecca said, "Hi, Alberto. Is everything OK?"

2. Alberto asked, "Can we go some place and talk?"

3. "Have you ever tried skiing?" he asked.

4. "No, it's not my thing," she answered.

5. Alberto said, "Our relationship is a friendship, right?"

2. Match the two parts of each sentence. Write the letters.

1. __d__ He said,

2. ____ I asked,

3. ____ "The test will be on Friday,"

4. ____ They said,

5. ____ "Are you married?"

a. the teacher said.

b. he asked.

c. "When is the party?"

✔**d.** "I haven't been there."

e. "Take us to your leader."

3. Add the correct punctuation to these sentences.

1. "This is a great book," I said.

2. I would love to read it   she said

3. I asked   Do you like science fiction books

4. I love them   she answered

5. Have you read anything else by this author   I asked

6. She answered   No, I haven't

4. Write an answer to each question below. Write sentences with direct speech. Use your own words.

1. He asked, "Would you like something to eat?"   _I said, "Yes, I would. Thanks."_

2. She asked, "When will you be back?"   _____

3. They asked, "Did he go to college?"   _____

4. She asked, "Why did you do that?"   _____

5. I asked, "Will you marry me?"   _____

POWER Practice

5. Think of an important conversation from your past. Write five sentences from that conversation below. Use direct speech.

Examples: The manager asked, "Do you want the job?"
I said, "It sounds very interesting."

1. _____

2. _____

3. _____

4. _____

5. _____

6. What do you and your friends often talk about? Write five sentences from a typical conversation. Use direct speech. Use your own paper.

Examples: Carol said, "That was a great party this weekend."
"I had to study," I said.

INDIRECT SPEECH

DIRECT SPEECH		INDIRECT SPEECH		
R **E** **V** "They are living in L.A." **I** "We need your help." **E** "I bought a car." **W**	**SUBJECT**	**PRESENT TENSE VERB**	**(THAT)**	**REPORT**
	She They	says say	(that)	they **are living** in L.A. they **need** our help. she **bought** a car.
	SUBJECT	**PAST TENSE VERB**	**(THAT)**	**REPORT**
	She They	said answered	(that)	they **were living** in L.A. they **needed** our help. she **had bought** a car.

📝 NOTES

- A sentence with indirect speech is a report of a person's statement.
- A sentence with indirect speech has a verb like **say**, **answer**, **suggest**, or **tell**.
- If the verb **say/answer** is in the present tense, then the report is in the same tense as the person's exact words.
- If the verb **say/answer** is in the past tense, then there is often a shift of tense in the report. Verbs in the present tense shift to the past, and verbs in the past tense shift to the past perfect.
- We can also use the simple past tense instead of the past perfect tense in indirect speech: *She said she bought a car* instead of *She said she had bought a car.*
- We sometimes have to change the pronouns and adverbs the speaker used in direct speech when we report the statement in indirect speech: *She said, "I'm working now." She said she was working then.*

Rebecca **said that** Alberto **had given** her the photo.

Practice

7. Underline the sentences with indirect speech.

<u>Ramón said he had something for his brother.</u> Alberto said, "Thanks. I can really use these goggles." Ramón asked, "Is Rebecca going with you?" Alberto said that Rebecca didn't want to go. He said that Rebecca wanted to spend Christmas in San Francisco.

Nancy asked Rebecca, "What's this?" Rebecca answered that it was a photo of Ramón and Alex. She said Alberto had given it to her. Nancy suggested that Alberto was trying to tell Rebecca something.

8. Match the direct speech with the correct indirect speech.

1. __c__ Lisa says, "I like Chicago."   **a.** She said she was living in Chicago.

2. _____ Lisa says, "I live in Chicago."   **b.** She said she had lived in Chicago.

3. _____ Lisa said, "I live in Chicago."   ✔**c.** She says she likes Chicago.

4. _____ Lisa said, "I'm living in Chicago."   **d.** She said she lived in Chicago.

5. _____ Lisa said, "I lived in Chicago."   **e.** She says she lives in Chicago.

9. Write the correct verb forms in the sentences below.

1. He said, "I'm bored."   He said that he __was__ bored.

2. They said, "We have a problem."   They said that they _____ a problem.

3. I answered, "We're leaving."   I answered that we _____.

4. They said, "He isn't coming."   They said that he _____.

5. She said, "He took a taxi."   She said he _____ a taxi.

6. We said, "We don't want to do it."   We said we _____ to do it.

7. I said, "I didn't see him."   I said that I _____ him.

10. Rewrite the direct speech below as indirect speech.

1. He said, "I'm hungry."   He said that he was hungry.

2. You said, "I want to go."   _____

3. "I'm feeling sick," I said.   _____

4. "I studied all night," she answered.   _____

5. They say, "We love pizza."   _____

6. He says, "It's a great movie."   _____

POWER Practice

11. What have you said to people today? Write five sentences with indirect speech.

Examples: *I said I needed a vacation.*
             I said that indirect speech was hard.

1. _____

2. _____

3. _____

4. _____

5. _____

12. Think of people who are important to you. What have they said to you? Write five sentences with indirect speech. Use your own paper.

Examples: *My grandfather said that he was proud of me.*
             My sister said she'd written me a letter.

EMBEDDED QUESTIONS

DIRECT SPEECH	MAIN CLAUSE	EMBEDDED QUESTION		
YES/NO QUESTIONS	**PRESENT TENSE**	**IF/ WHETHER**	**SUBJECT**	**VERB**
"Are you coming?"	She's **asking** you	if	you	are coming.
"Did he leave?"	They **want** to know	whether	he	left.
WH- QUESTIONS		**WH- QUESTION WORD (+ SUBJECT)**		**VERB**
"Who is coming?"		who		is coming.
"When did he leave?"		when he		left.
	PAST TENSE	**IF/ WHETHER**	**SUBJECT**	**VERB**
	She's **asked** you	if	you	were coming.
	They **wanted** to know	whether	he	had left.
		WH- QUESTION WORD (+ SUBJECT)		**VERB**
		who		was coming.
		when he		had left.

NOTES

- A sentence with an embedded question is a report of a person's question.
- An embedded **Yes/No** question uses [**if/whether** + subject + verb]: *He asked if I wanted coffee.*
- An embedded **Wh-** question uses [**Wh-** question word + (subject +) verb]: *They asked who did it.*
- If the verb in the main clause is in the *present* tense, the embedded question is in the same tense as the person's exact words.
- If the verb in the main clause is in the *past* tense, there is often a shift of tense in the embedded question.
- We use a question mark after an embedded question only when the main clause is a question: *Do you know who she is?*

Rebecca **asked** Alex **if he'd had a good Christmas**.

Practice

13. Check (✔) the sentences with embedded questions. Underline the embedded question.

1. ✔ Did Ramón ask <u>if Rebecca could join him for Christmas</u>?

2. _____ Rebecca wanted to know whether Ramón had talked to Alex.

3. _____ "Have you heard from your brother?" asked Ramón.

4. _____ Ramón asked Rebecca what she wanted to drink.

5. _____ On the phone, Ramón asked Alex what he'd received for Christmas.

6. _____ Did Rebecca ask if she could speak to Alex?

7. _____ Did Alex ask Rebecca if he could continue his guitar lessons?

14. Make sentences with words from each box.

They are asking I asked	if	what	he bought for her she is going
I want to know We wanted to know	whether	where	you had been there it costs
		how much	

1. <u>I want to know where she is going.</u>

2. _____

3. _____

4. _____

5. _____

15. Write the verbs in the embedded questions.

1. ("Where did you learn English?") Does the teacher know where you <u>learned</u> English?

2. ("Who won the game?") She asked who _____ the game.

3. ("When did she call?") He wanted to know when she _____.

4. ("Did you finish the work?") I asked if you _____ the work.

5. ("How do you do it?") He asked her how she _____ it.

6. ("Does the car need gas?") Do you know whether the car _____ gas?

POWER Practice

16. Think about questions you have asked lately. Complete the sentences below.

Examples: I asked my friend Yoshi if he wanted to get some pizza. I asked my teacher when our exam was.

1. I asked _____ if _____

2. I asked _____ whether _____

3. I asked _____ when _____

4. I asked _____ who _____

17. What questions have your family members asked this week? Write five sentences with embedded questions. After each sentence, write the person's exact words in parentheses. Use your own paper.

Example: My brother asked if he could borrow my car. ("Can I borrow your car?")

REVIEW: DIRECT OBJECT GERUNDS

	MAIN VERB	DIRECT OBJECT GERUND	
He	hates	**driving**	in bad weather.
We didn't	like	**living**	there.
Have you	finished	**doing**	your homework?
When did you	quit	**working**?	

📝 NOTES

- A gerund is [verb + **-ing**].
- We use a gerund in place of a noun to name a situation or an action.
- A direct object gerund follows the main verb in a sentence: *We continued practicing. Do you enjoy skating?*
- A direct object gerund can also have words after it: *We continued practicing for two more hours.*
- Some common verbs with direct object gerunds are **avoid, begin, consider, continue, discuss, enjoy, finish, hate, like, love, practice, quit,** and **start**.

Ramón enjoyed **listening** to Rebecca's song.

Practice

1. Check (✔) the sentences with direct object gerunds. Underline the gerunds.

1. __✔__ Rebecca and Ramón like <u>giving</u> presents.

2. _____ Rebecca loved Ramón's gift.

3. _____ Did Ramón and Rebecca discuss spending New Year's Eve together?

4. _____ The Caseys were playing a game.

5. _____ Kevin doesn't like celebrating Christmas without Rebecca.

6. _____ Kevin plans to visit Rebecca in San Francisco.

2. Complete each sentence with a direct object gerund. Use your own words.

1. He finished ___reading___ the book.

2. She likes _____ her car.

3. Does he like _____ soccer?

4. She started _____ every day.

5. They discussed _____ to Brazil.

6. I didn't begin _____ until 9:00.

3. Complete each sentence with a main verb. Use your own words.

1. She _____began_____ complaining about the weather.

2. They _____ taking a vacation.

3. He doesn't _____ eating alone.

4. She _____ talking to her old boyfriend.

5. Did he _____ seeing a psychologist?

6. When will she _____ exercising?

4. Write statements or questions with the words in parentheses. Use any tense. Use direct object gerunds.

1. (love + take photos) I used to love taking photos. _____

2. (start + clean the house) _____

3. (finish + write the book) _____

4. (like + work with children) _____

5. (avoid + go to the doctor) _____

6. (discuss + get married) _____

POWER Practice

5. What are your likes and dislikes? Write five sentences with direct object gerunds.

Examples: *I enjoy reading long books.*
I hate waking up early.

1. _____

2. _____

3. _____

4. _____

5. _____

6. What does your friend like or dislike? Write five questions with direct object gerunds to ask him/her. Use your own paper.

Example: *Do you like walking in the rain?*

REVIEW: DIRECT OBJECT INFINITIVES

	MAIN VERB	DIRECT OBJECT INFINITIVE	
They	like	**to watch**	movies.
I don't	want	**to forget**.	
Did you	promise	**to help**	them?
When did they	decide	**to go**	there?

NOTES

- An infinitive is [**to** + simple form of verb].
- An infinitive can be the direct object of the main verb in a sentence. It follows the verb: *We continued to talk. Do you like to sing?*
- A direct object infinitive can also have words after it: *We continued to talk for two hours.*
- Some common verbs with direct object infinitives are **begin**, **continue**, **decide**, **hate**, **hope**, **learn**, **like**, **love**, **need**, **offer**, **plan**, **promise**, **refuse**, **start**, and **want**.

Ramón: *I need **to be** at the restaurant for New Year's Eve. Would you like **to come**?*

Rebecca: *Thanks. I'd love **to come**.*

Practice

7. Underline the direct object infinitives.

Rebecca and Ramón started to kiss, but Nancy walked in. They talked with her for a little while, and then Ramón needed to leave. Rebecca wanted to say good-night, so she went to the door with him. He told her that he needed to be at the restaurant for New Year's Eve, and she promised to be there, too. They're planning to begin the new year together.

8. Put the words in order. Write questions with direct object infinitives.

1. take / he / more / to / classes / need / does   _Does he need to take more classes?_

2. where / cook / you / did / learn / to   _____

3. medicine / do / want / study / you / to   _____

4. you / leave / to / did / decide / when   _____

5. plan / does / college / she / to / to / go   _____

6. why / you / to / need / do / leave   _____

7. want / to / do / you / what / see   _____

8. she / where / did / go / decide / to   _____

9. did / promise / come / home / he / to   _____

10. will / refuse / they / to / speak   _____

9. Complete the sentences with the words from the box.

to buy	to do	to ride	to talk	to watch	✔ to win

1. She wants _to win_ the game.

2. Does she like _____ baseball?

3. He refuses _____ expensive shoes.

4. They continued _____ for hours.

5. When does he need _____ the work?

6. When did you learn _____ a horse?

10. Complete the sentences. Use your own words.

1. Cats love _to sleep in a warm place._

2. The players are hoping _____

3. The children wanted _____

4. The dog refused _____

5. Her boyfriend promised _____

6. I'm learning _____

POWER Practice

11. PRETEND: You are making New Year's resolutions. Complete the sentences with direct object infinitives.

Examples: *I will begin to exercise regularly.*

I plan to study more.

1. I will begin _____

2. I plan _____

3. I promise _____

4. I've decided _____

5. I'm going to learn _____

12. PRETEND: You are interviewing the leader of your country. Write five questions with direct object infinitives. Use your own paper.

Examples: *Do you plan to do something about crime?*

When did you decide to enter politics?

DIRECT OBJECT INFINITIVES WITH SUBJECTS

	MAIN VERB	SECOND SUBJECT	DIRECT OBJECT INFINITIVE	
He	asked	**her**	**to dance**.	
They don't	allow	**people**	**to swim**	there.
Does she	expect	**her brother and sister**	**to come**	to the wedding?
Who	convinced	**them**	**to try**	it?

📝 NOTES

- A direct object infinitive can have a subject that is different from the subject of the main verb.
- If the subject of a direct object infinitive is a pronoun, we use the object form: **me**, **us**, **you**, **them**, **him**, **her**, or **it**.
- Some common verbs that take a direct object infinitive with a second subject are: **allow**, **ask**, **convince**, **expect**, **invite**, **order**, **like**, **need**, **permit**, **teach**, **tell**, and **want**.

Rebecca wants **Kevin to come** to San Francisco.

Practice

13. Underline the subjects of the direct object infinitives. Circle the direct object infinitives.

1. Alex wanted Rebecca to have a statue of "Mighty Casey."

2. Ramón helped Rebecca to rebuild the fire.

3. Rebecca told Ramón to put his hand under cold water.

4. Ramón invited Rebecca to come to the restaurant on New Year's Eve.

5. Brendan and Anne convinced Kevin to go to San Francisco.

6. They want Rebecca and Kevin to be together.

14. Rewrite the sentences. Use an object pronoun in place of the boldfaced words.

1. He wants **my sister and me** to come.   He wants us to come.

2. She taught **the dog** to do it.   _____

3. They needed **Louisa** to bring the book.   _____

4. He has invited **Mr. Smith** to go to lunch.   _____

5. We are helping **the children** to learn the game.   _____

6. They've asked **our group** to sing.   _____

15. Make sentences with words from each box.

I	He	will ask	me	him		try it
You	She	convinced	you	her	to	dance
We	They	expected	us	them		do a good job
		didn't teach				get married

1. *She expected me to do a good job.*

2. _____

3. _____

4. _____

5. _____

6. _____

16. Complete the sentences. Use a second subject with a direct object infinitive.

1. He said to me, "You have to come." He expected *me to come.*

2. She asked me, "Could you pass the salt?" She asked _____

3. They said to you, "Close the door." They told _____

4. The general said to the soldier, "Stand up." The general ordered _____

5. The woman said to the girl, "Please get help." The woman asked _____

6. The teacher said to us, "Study hard." The teacher wanted _____

7. Her father said to her, "You can go to the party." Her father allowed _____

 Practice

17. Describe your relationship with a close friend. Write six sentences with direct object infinitives with subjects. Use your own paper.

Examples: I expect him to be honest with me. She likes me to make all the decisions.

18. What do your parents expect you to be or to do? Write six sentences with direct object infinitives. Use the verbs *expect, want, ask, allow,* or *tell.*
Use your own paper.

Examples: My parents expect me to study hard.
They want me to be happy.

PASSIVE VOICE: SIMPLE PRESENT TENSE, AFFIRMATIVE AND NEGATIVE STATEMENTS

AFFIRMATIVE STATEMENTS

SUBJECT	BE	PAST PARTICIPLE	
I	am	invited	to many parties.
Spanish	is	spoken	here.
Oranges	are	grown	in warm climates.

NEGATIVE STATEMENTS

SUBJECT	BE + NOT	PAST PARTICIPLE	
I	am not	invited	to many weddings.
Spanish	is not isn't	spoken	there.
Oranges	are not aren't	grown	in cold climates.

 NOTES

- The subject of an active voice sentence is the *doer* of an action: *Somebody washes the floors at night.* (*Somebody* is the subject.)
- The subject of a passive voice sentence is the *receiver* of an action: *The floors are washed at night.* (*The floors* is the subject.)
- We often use the passive voice when we do not know the doer of an action. We also use the passive voice when information about the doer is not important.
- We use [subject + auxiliary verb **am/is/are** (+ **not**) + past participle of main verb] in passive voice, simple present tense statements.
- Regular past participles are [simple form of verb + **-ed** or **-d**].
- Some common irregular past participles are **begun, built, caught, done, grown, held, kept, made, seen, sold, spent, spoken,** and **taught.**

Rebecca's song **is recorded** at the recording studio.

Practice

1. Underline the verbs in the passive voice, simple present tense.

Kevin comes to San Francisco to visit Rebecca. He <u>is invited</u> to her recording session. At the studio, he and her friends are introduced to each other. Kevin is invited to sit in the control room, and the rehearsal is begun. Rebecca sings "Dreamcatcher." She is accompanied by several musicians. The recording is made, and Rebecca is congratulated by everyone in the studio.

2. Match the passive voice and active voice sentences with the same meaning.

Passive Voice Statements

1. __d__ A lot of corn is grown here.
2. _____ The streets are cleaned at night.
3. _____ Snacks are not permitted in class.
4. _____ The local news is reported on TV.
5. _____ Several languages are taught there.

Active Voice Statements

a. Somebody reports the local news on TV.
b. Teachers don't permit snacks in class.
c. Teachers there teach several languages.
✔d. People grow a lot of corn here.
e. Somebody cleans the streets at night.

3. Rewrite these passive sentences as active sentences. Use *People* + the simple present tense.

1. Many fish are caught in that lake.   *People catch many fish in that lake.*

2. English is spoken here.   _____

3. Baseball isn't played there.   _____

4. Bananas aren't grown in Alaska.   _____

5. Computers are used in schools.   _____

4. Put the words in order. Write passive voice sentences.

1. Brazil / spoken / in / Portuguese / is   *Portuguese is spoken in Brazil.*

2. trash / is / on / collected / the / Fridays   _____

3. sold / store / newspapers / in / are / that   _____

4. is / parking / allowed / not / here   _____

5. Complete the sentences. Write the verbs in the passive voice, simple present tense.

1. People eat pasta in Italy.   Pasta *is eaten* _____ in Italy.

2. People don't speak Spanish there.   Spanish _____ there.

3. Somebody washes the blackboards after school.   The blackboards _____ after school.

4. People make movies in Hollywood.   Movies _____ in Hollywood.

5. Somebody delivers the mail before noon.   The mail _____ before noon.

6. People don't use computers there.   Computers _____ there.

POWER Practice

6. Complete the following active voice sentences about your home country. Then rewrite each sentence in the passive voice.

Example: *People speak Spanish in my country. Spanish is spoken in my country.*

1. People speak _____ in my country. _____

2. People often eat _____ there. _____

3. People usually build houses of _____. _____

4. People produce _____. _____

5. People play _____. _____

PASSIVE VOICE: SIMPLE PRESENT TENSE, *YES/NO* QUESTIONS AND SHORT ANSWERS

BE	SUBJECT	PAST PARTICIPLE	
Am	I	invited?	
Is	Spanish	spoken	here?
Are	oranges	grown	there?

AFFIRMATIVE SHORT ANSWERS		
Yes,	you **are**.	
	it **is**.	
	they **are**.	

NEGATIVE SHORT ANSWERS		
No,	You **are not**. You're **not**./you **aren't**.	
	it **is not**. it's **not**./it **isn't**.	
	they **are not**. they're **not**./they **aren't**.	

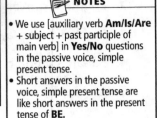

NOTES
- We use [auxiliary verb **Am/Is/Are** + subject + past participle of main verb] in **Yes/No** questions in the passive voice, simple present tense.
- Short answers in the passive voice, simple present tense are like short answers in the present tense of **BE**.

Is guitar practice **encouraged** at Vincent's house?

Yes, it **is**.

Practice

7. Check (✔) the *Yes/No* questions in the passive voice, simple present tense.

1. ✔ Is Alex taken to Vincent's house?

2. _____ Is he invited to go to Vincent's room?

3. _____ Do the boys practice together?

4. _____ Do they talk about Taiwan?

5. _____ Is English spoken in Taiwan?

6. _____ Are the boys allowed to make their own plans?

7. _____ Are they making New Year's Eve plans?

8. _____ Is Vincent's money kept in a piggy bank?

8. Put the words in order. Write *Yes/No* questions in the passive voice, simple present tense.

1. factory / in / are / that / used / computers
   Are computers used in that factory?

2. your / soccer / country / played / is / in
   _____

3. those / made / hand / by / are / sweaters
   _____

4. needed / am / home / at / I
   _____

5. cameras / in / allowed / the / are / museum
   _____

6. store / candy / is / sold / at / that
   _____

9. Change these statements to **Yes/No** questions. Write short answers.

1. Baseball isn't played much there. _Is baseball played much there? No, it isn't._ _____

2. Honey is made by bees. _____

3. Drivers are required to pass a test. _____

4. The house is built of wood. _____

5. Experiments are done in that lab. _____

6. Visitors are not allowed in that area. _____

7. Elections are held every four years. _____

10. Write **Yes/No** questions about Christmas in San Francisco. Use the passive voice, simple present tense.

1. Christmas / (celebrate) / in San Francisco   _Is Christmas celebrated in San Francisco?_

2. the day / (spend) / at home   _____

3. the city / (decorate) / with Christmas lights   _____

4. businesses / (close) / for the day   _____

5. special foods / (prepare) / for Christmas dinner   _____

6. presents / (exchange) / among friends   _____

11. Write **Yes/No** questions in the passive voice, simple present tense.

1. _Are concerts held outdoors sometimes?_   Yes, people hold concerts outdoors sometimes.

2. _____   Yes, they sell magazines in that store.

3. _____   No, people don't grow coffee in Canada.

4. _____   No, they don't allow food in the computer lab.

5. _____   Yes, people build houses of stone sometimes.

6. _____   Yes, people pronounce "said" like "red".

POWER Practice

12. Write questions to ask a friend about his/her home country. Look at the passive statements you wrote about your country in Exercise 6. Change them to **Yes/No** questions for your friend. Use your own paper.

Example: *Is Spanish spoken in your country?*

PREPOSITIONAL PHRASES WITH *BY* IN PASSIVE VOICE STATEMENTS

	PASSIVE VOICE, SIMPLE PRESENT TENSE	PREPOSITIONAL PHRASE WITH *BY*	
		BY	AGENT
AFFIRMATIVE STATEMENTS	These programs are organized		**the United Nations.**
NEGATIVE STATEMENTS	Rice isn't grown	**by**	**farmers in this area.**
YES / NO QUESTIONS	Is Spanish spoken		**many people?**

NOTES
- We can name the doer of an action (the *agent*) in a prepositional phrase with **by** if this information is necessary or important.
- We can use a prepositional phrase [**by** + agent] after the past participle of the main verb.

Bill has decided to quit school.
Rebecca is surprised **by his news**.

Practice

13. Check (✔) the passive sentences with [*by* + agent].

1. ___✔___ Rebecca is surprised by Bill's news.

2. _____ She is shocked by Bill's decision to quit.

3. _____ Bill says he knows some musicians in Los Angeles.

4. _____ Many musicians are employed by the record industry there.

5. _____ Bill is expected by his friends in L.A.

6. _____ Rebecca and Bill are going to miss each other.

14. Choose the correct prepositional phrase with *by* for each sentence. Write the letter.

1. __b__ Speeding drivers are stopped   **a.** by artists.

2. _____ Taxes are collected   ✔**b.** by the police.

3. _____ Children are taught   **c.** by farmers.

4. _____ Pictures are painted   **d.** by the government.

5. _____ Vegetables are grown   **e.** by actors.

6. _____ Plays are performed   **f.** by mechanics.

7. _____ Cars are repaired   **g.** by teachers.

15. Add a prepositional phrase with *by* to each passive voice sentence.

1. Representatives are elected every two years <u>by the voters.</u>

2. French is spoken in France _____

3. Calculus is taught in high schools _____

4. The mail is delivered around 10:00 A.M. _____

5. Coffee is grown in Brazil _____

16. Look at the prepositional phrases with *by* in these sentences. Do they supply necessary information? Check (✔) *Necessary* or *Unnecessary*. Cross out the unnecessary phrases.

	NECESSARY	UNNECESSARY
1. The company is owned by his family.	✔	
2. Spanish is spoken ~~by people~~ in Peru.		✔
3. Christmas is celebrated by people on December 25.		
4. The food at that restaurant is served by singing waiters.		
5. The English word "eye" is pronounced like "I" by people.		
6. Math is taught by teachers in all the schools.		

17. Change the sentences from active voice to passive voice. Include the prepositional phrase with *by* only when it is necessary.

1. People don't grow corn in this area. <u>Corn isn't grown in this area.</u>

2. His mother makes his sweaters. <u>His sweaters are made by his mother.</u>

3. The boss makes all the decisions. _____

4. The college doesn't allow food in the college library. _____

5. The state holds state elections in November. _____

6. The school provides hot lunches. _____

POWER Practice

18. Write six passive voice statements about sports in your home country. Use the verbs *play, watch, enjoy,* and *prefer* or your own words. Include prepositional phrases with *by*. Use your own paper.

Examples: Sports are enjoyed by both men and women. Soccer is watched by millions of people.

THE LOST BOYS

PASSIVE VOICE: SIMPLE PAST TENSE, AFFIRMATIVE AND NEGATIVE STATEMENTS

AFFIRMATIVE STATEMENTS			
SUBJECT	**WAS/ WERE**	**PAST PARTICIPLE**	
The mail	**was**	**delivered**	this morning.
The tomatoes	**were**	**grown**	in his garden.

NEGATIVE STATEMENTS			
SUBJECT	**WAS / WERE + NOT**	**PAST PARTICIPLE**	
The package	**was not wasn't**	**delivered**	this morning.
The beans	**were not weren't**	**grown**	in his garden.

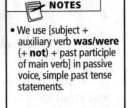

NOTES

• We use [subject + auxiliary verb **was/were** (+ **not**) + past participle of main verb] in passive voice, simple past tense statements.

Alex showed Vincent an ad for the skating rink.
The ad **was taken** from the newspaper.

Practice

1. Underline the verbs in the passive voice, simple past tense.

Vincent emptied his piggy bank and left the house. Outside, he <u>was met</u> by Alex, and the boys left to go ice skating. Their parents were not told about this plan. Soon the empty bank was noticed by Mrs. Wang, and she started looking for Vincent. Meanwhile, Rebecca took Kevin to the Mendozas' restaurant, and he and Ramón were introduced. They talked about Ramón's New Year's Eve party, and Kevin was invited to come. Then Mr. Wang came in. Rebecca was disturbed by the look on his face. Something was wrong.

2. Match the passive voice and active voice sentences with the same meaning.

1. __e__ His car was stolen last week.

2. _____ These bills were paid.

3. _____ He was not elected again.

4. _____ This photo was taken last year.

5. _____ We weren't invited to those parties.

a. People didn't elect him again.

b. Somebody took this photo last year.

c. Somebody paid these bills.

d. People didn't invite us to those parties.

✔ **e.** Somebody stole his car last week.

3. Complete the sentences. Use **wasn't / weren't** + the past participle of the verb in parentheses.

1. (keep) The money _wasn't kept_ _____ in a safe place.

2. (build) That house _____ with good materials.

3. (pay) The workers _____ very much.

4. (make) These gloves _____ in Italy.

5. (sell) The used car _____ for much money.

4. Change the sentences to passive voice. Do not use a prepositional phrase with **by**.

1. Somebody took my pen. _My pen was taken._ _____

2. Somebody invented the bicycle in France. _____

3. Somebody grew these oranges in Florida. _____

4. People built this store in 1880. _____

5. People made these toys in Taiwan. _____

5. Change the sentences to passive voice. Use a prepositional phrase with **by** if necessary.

1. Somebody reported the fires on the 6:00 news. _The fires were reported on the 6:00 news._

2. My father didn't paint that picture. _That picture wasn't painted by my father._ _____

3. A car hit our cat. _____

4. Somebody ate all the cookies. _____

5. Somebody took the man to the hospital. _____

6. Thomas Edison didn't invent the telephone. _____

POWER Practice

6. Answer the questions with passive voice statements in the simple past tense.

Example: *Who named you?* *I was named by my parents.*

1. Where were you born? _____

2. When were you born? _____

3. Where were you raised? _____

4. Who raised you? _____

PASSIVE VOICE: SIMPLE PAST TENSE, *YES/NO* QUESTIONS AND SHORT ANSWERS

WAS/ WERE	SUBJECT	PAST PARTICIPLE	
Was	the mail	**delivered**?	
Were	the tomatoes	**grown**	here?

SHORT ANSWERS		
YES/NO	**SUBJECT**	**WAS / WERE (+ NOT)**
Yes,	it	**was.**
No,		**was not./wasn't.**
Yes,	they	**were.**
No,		**were not./weren't.**

> **NOTES**
> • We use [auxiliary verb **Was/Were** + subject + past participle of main verb] in **Yes/ No** questions in the passive voice, simple past tense.
> • Short answers in the passive voice, simple past tense are like short answers in the past tense of **BE**.

Were the boys **seen** by a man at the skating rink?
Yes, they **were**.

Practice

7. Check (✔) the *Yes/No* questions in the passive voice, simple past tense.

1. **✔** Was Ramón surprised by Mr. Wang's questions?

2. _____ Were the boys found at Alex's house?

3. _____ Were the boys at the skating rink?

4. _____ Was Alex tripped by another skater?

5. _____ Were Ramón and Rebecca looking for the boys?

6. _____ Were Alex and Vincent seen by anyone at the skating rink?

8. Put the words in order. Write *Yes/No* questions in the passive voice, simple past tense.

1. job / done / on / the / was / time *Was the job done on time?* _____

2. to / was / the / he / party / invited _____

3. you / caught / were / rain / in / the _____

4. were / eaten / the / all / chocolates _____

5. English / was / your / high school / at / taught _____

6. letters / post office / the / to / taken / were / the _____

7. winner / speech / the / give / to / asked / was / the _____

8. was / baby / the / after / father / his / named _____

9. Complete the **Yes/No** questions. Use the verbs in parentheses. Use the passive voice, simple past tense.

1. (invent) __Was_____ the automobile __invented_____ in the 1800s?

2. (deliver) _____ the mail _____ this morning?

3. (cancel) _____ classes _____ because of the snow?

4. (report) _____ the story _____ on the news?

5. (destroy) _____ any homes _____ in the fire?

10. Change statements 1–6 to **Yes/No** questions in the passive voice, simple past tense. Write short answers.

   This summer I had fun on the 4th of July. **(1)** I was invited to a cookout at the house of some friends. **(2)** I was introduced to many new people there. Too many! But it wasn't a problem. **(3)** I wasn't expected to remember all their names. **(4)** A lot of good food was prepared for the party. **(5)** Hamburgers were cooked on the grill. There were many kinds of vegetables, breads, salads, and desserts. **(6)** All the food was eaten by the time I left.

1. __Were you invited to a cookout?   Yes, I was._____

2. _____

3. _____

4. _____

5. _____

6. _____

11. Write **Yes/No** questions. Use the passive voice, simple past tense

1. *Romeo and Juliet* / (write) / by Shakespeare __Was Romeo and Juliet written by Shakespeare?__

2. anyone / (hurt) / in the accident _____

3. the Olympic Games / (hold) / last year _____

4. the Suez Canal / (build) / in the 1800s _____

5. you / (see) / by a doctor _____

12. Write eight **Yes/No** questions for a friend. Use the passive voice, simple past tense. Use the past participles in the box. Use your own paper.

born	educated	expected	named	raised

Examples: *Were you born in this country?   Were you named after someone?*

TRANSITIVE AND INTRANSITIVE VERBS

	TRANSITIVE VERBS			
A	**SUBJECT**	**VERB**	**DIRECT OBJECT**	
C	People	**speak**	**Spanish**	here.
T	Many people	**enjoy**	**swimming.**	
I	Somebody	**stole**	**my bicycle.**	
V	They	**invited**	**us.**	
E	**SUBJECT**	**VERB**		
P	Spanish	**is spoken**	here.	
A	Swimming	**is enjoyed**	by many people.	
S	My bicycle	**was stolen.**		
S	We	**were invited.**		
I				
V				
E				

	INTRANSITIVE VERBS	
A	**SUBJECT**	**VERB**
C	People	**talk.**
T	Many people	**swim.**
I	Somebody	**shouted.**
V	They	**waited.**
E		
P		
A		NONE
S		
S		
I		
V		
E		

📝 **NOTES**

- Transitive verbs are followed by direct objects.
- Intransitive verbs are not followed by direct objects.
- Most transitive verbs can be used in either the active or the passive voice.
- Intransitive verbs are used in the active voice only. Some common intransitive verbs are: **be, belong, come, go, happen, laugh, listen, live, sleep, smile,** and **work.**
- Some verbs can be either transitive or intransitive: *He's reading a book. He's reading. / Let's begin the game. Let's begin. / Stop that noise! Stop!*

Kevin **makes a phone call**, and Monica **listens.**

Practice

13. Underline the transitive verbs and their direct objects. Circle the intransitive verbs.

Rebecca and Ramón <u>discuss Alex</u>. Ramón (is) upset with him and worried about him. Ramón calls Kevin, but there is no news. The babysitter comes to the door, and Kevin explains the situation. Monica waits while Kevin calls Mrs. Wang. He gets some good news: the boys have phoned. They are at the hospital.

14. Write *T* next to statements with transitive verbs and *I* next to statements with intransitive verbs.

1. __T__ Monica was hired by Ramón.

2. __I__ She came to the door.

3. ____ She arrived on time.

4. ____ Kevin heard the doorbell.

5. ____ He went to the door.

6. ____ He opened it.

7. ____ Monica introduced herself.

8. ____ The situation was explained by Kevin.

9. ____ He called Mrs. Wang.

10. ____ Mrs. Wang gave him the news.

11. ____ Monica listened.

12. ____ The news shocked them.

15. Put a period after each intransitive verb. Write a direct object after each transitive verb, and then put a period after it.

1. The baby slept ._____

2. We saw _a movie._____

3. I wore _____

4. Everyone laughed _____

5. He isn't working _____

6. Somebody stole _____

7. Something happened _____

8. I bought _____

16. Change these sentences from active voice to passive voice if it is possible. If the verb is intransitive, write *intransitive*.

1. They made our TV in Japan. _Our TV was made in Japan._____

2. That car didn't belong to him. _intransitive_____

3. I slept late on Sunday. _____

4. They collected the trash yesterday. _____

5. It happened last Thursday. _____

6. A car hit their dog. _____

17. Write one active voice and one passive voice sentence with each *transitive* verb. Write only an active voice sentence with each *intransitive* verb. Use the simple past tense.

ACTIVE VOICE:	PASSIVE VOICE:
1. (build) _My neighbors built a house._	_The school was built in 1950._
2. (go) _I went downtown._	_(no passive)_
3. (hit) _____	_____
4. (invite) _____	_____
5. (listen) _____	_____
6. (make) _____	_____
7. (smile) _____	_____

Practice

18. Write eight sentences about the first ten years of your life. Use transitive and intransitive verbs. Use both the active and the passive voice. Use your own paper.

Examples: I was born in Seoul. We lived in a small apartment.

REVIEW: PRESENT CONDITIONAL STATEMENTS

IF CLAUSE	RESULT CLAUSE
If I **excercise** every day,	I **feel** better.
If he **needs** help,	**then** he **asks** his brother.

RESULT CLAUSE	IF CLAUSE
I **don't work** well	if I **don't get** enough sleep.
We **eat** outside	if it **doesn't rain**.

📝 **NOTES**

- A present conditional sentence tells the reason for a result. It has two clauses.
- The **if** clause tells the reason. The result clause tells the result.
- We use present tense verb forms in both the **if** clause and the result clause.
- The **if** clause can come before or after the result clause.
- We use a comma after an **if** clause at the beginning of a sentence.
- We sometimes use **then** at the beginning of the result clause when the result clause follows the **if** clause.

Mr. Wang: **If** children **do not obey** their parents, **then** their parents **do not trust** them.

Practice

1. Check (✔) the present conditional sentences. Underline the **if** clause and circle the result clause.

1. ✔ If children are missing, (their parents become very worried.)

2. _____ Ramón and Rebecca are looking in the park for the missing boys.

3. _____ Alex sometimes takes a shortcut through the park if he walks home.

4. _____ Mr. and Mrs. Wang found Vincent and Alex when they got to the hospital.

5. _____ If Vincent behaves badly, then his father thinks he is not trustworthy.

6. _____ If children get into trouble, their parents have to help them.

2. Complete the sentences. Write **if** or **then**.

1. _____If_____ I don't eat right, _____then_____ I don't feel well.

2. You can't concentrate _____ you feel sleepy.

3. _____ the spring rains are heavy, _____ there are floods.

4. They cancel school _____ there is a bad snowstorm.

5. He doesn't have breakfast _____ there isn't time.

6. _____ I take the shortcut, _____ I save five minutes.

3. Complete the sentences. Use the simple present tense of the verb in parentheses.

1. (have) If I _____have_____ time, I like to walk along the river.

2. (make) I do the dishes if my roommate _____ dinner.

3. (read, not) He _____ the morning paper if he doesn't have time.

4. (sit) They always _____ up front if there is space.

5. (be, not) If it's a holiday, then the stores _____ open.

4. Complete the sentences with your own words. Write *if* clauses or result clauses.

1. Students usually get poor grades _if they don't study._

2. If the classroom is too warm, _students feel sleepy._

3. People gain weight if _____

4. If traffic is bad, then _____

5. Some people become angry if _____

6. If there's a big sports event on TV, _____

7. Drivers slow down if _____

POWER Practice

5. Complete these sentences about you. Write result clauses.

Example: If I am lucky, there's an empty seat when I get on the bus.

1. If I am hungry, _____

2. If I don't get enough sleep, _____

3. If I need money, _____

4. If I see something I like in a store, _____

5. If I catch a cold, _____

6. What things do you like to do if you have time? Write six present conditional sentences. Use your own paper.

Examples: If I have time in the morning, I make a hot breakfast.
I watch TV in the evening if I don't have homework.

REVIEW: FUTURE CONDITIONAL STATEMENTS

IF CLAUSE	RESULT CLAUSE
If you **practice,**	you **will improve.**
If he **doesn't call** me,	then I**'ll call** him.
RESULT CLAUSE	**IF CLAUSE**
They**'ll come** with us	if we **invite** them.
We **won't be** able to go	if the car **doesn't work.**

📝 NOTES
• A future conditional sentence tells the reason for a result in the future.
• We use present tense verb forms in the **if** clause.
• We use the future with **will** in the result clause.
• The **if** clause can come before or after the result clause.
• We use a comma after an **if** clause at the beginning of a sentence.
• We sometimes use **then** at the beginning of the result clause when the result clause follows the **if** clause.

If it **is** best for Alex, Ramón **will send** him to live with his mother.

7. Check (✔) the future conditional sentences. Underline the verbs in the *if* clauses of those sentences, and circle the verbs in the result clauses.

1. ✔ If Alex has to choose between his parents, he will feel terrible.

2. _____ If parents get a divorce, it's usually painful for the children.

3. _____ If Ramón finds his son, he'll be very relieved.

4. _____ Ramón will send Alex to live with his mother if that is best for his son.

5. _____ It's hard on children if they have to go back and forth between their parents.

6. _____ Ramón will get some good news if he calls Kevin.

8. Complete the sentences. Use *will* + the verb in parentheses. Use affirmative and negative contractions.

1. (help) If you need me, I _'ll help_____ you.

2. (be) If we don't invite her, she _____ upset.

3. (call) I _____ you if I get home by 10:00 P.M.

4. (mind, not) He _____ if I borrow his bike.

5. (have, not) If you follow these directions, you _____ any trouble.

6. (give) They _____ us a raise if we do a good job.

7. (go, not) If you don't go, I _____ either.

8. (be) We _____ late if we don't hurry.

9. (improve) He _____ his English if he reads a lot.

9. Complete the sentences. Use the verbs in parentheses. Use contractions.

1. If he _____fails_____ (fail) this course, then he ___won't graduate___ (graduate, not).

2. If the car _____ (cost) too much, then I _____ (buy, not) it.

3. If she _____ (do) well in the interview, she _____ (get) the job.

4. If you _____ (be, not) ready in five minutes, we _____ (leave) without you!

5. I _____ (give) him the message if I _____ (see) him.

6. I _____ (be) disappointed if you _____ (come, not).

10. Complete the following sentences. Add an *if* clause or a result clause. Use your own words.

1. If it rains tomorrow, _they'll postpone the cookout._____

2. I'll have a snack later if _I'm hungry._____

3. If he doesn't study, _____

4. His friends will be surprised if _____

5. If she wins that trip to Disney World, _____

6. If we don't pay the rent, _____

7. You'll be successful if _____

8. Our team will win if _____

POWER Practice

11. Complete these future conditional sentences about you. Write *if* clauses.

Example: *I'll stay home tomorrow if I'm sick.*

1. I'll celebrate _____

2. I'll be disappointed _____

3. I'll be happy _____

4. I'll have a good time _____

5. I'll be successful _____

12. Write six future conditional sentences about you, your family, or your friends. Use your own paper.

Examples: *If my brother needs me, I'll do anything for him.*
My parents will be proud of me if I do well in school.

CONTRARY-TO-FACT CONDITIONAL STATEMENTS

IF CLAUSE				RESULT CLAUSE				
IF	SUBJECT	SIMPLE PAST TENSE VERB		(THEN)	SUBJECT	WOULD	SIMPLE FORM OF MAIN VERB	
	she	were	here,		she		tell	you the story.
If	I	had	time,	(then)	I	would	get	more exercise.
	we	didn't have	homework,		I		be	at the party now.

CONTRACTIONS WITH *WOULD*	
AFFIRMATIVE	
I'd, we'd, you'd, they'd, he'd, she'd, it'd	
NEGATIVE	
I, we, you, they, he, she, it	wouldn't

NOTES

- We use contrary-to-fact conditional sentences for unreal conditions in the present. Unreal conditions exist only in the imagination.
- We use the simple past tense in the **if** clause.
- We use **would** or a contraction with **would** in the result clause.
- The **if** clause can come before or after the result clause.
- We use **were** for **I, he, she**, and **it** as well as **we, you**, and **they** when we use **BE** in the **if** clause.
- Sometimes people use **was** with **I, he, she**, and **it** in conversation: *If she was here, she'd tell you the story.*

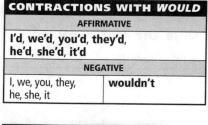

If Rebecca **weren't** with Ramón, she **wouldn't be** so happy.

Practice

13. Check (✔) the contrary-to-fact conditional sentences. Underline the verb in the **if** clause. Circle the verb in the result clause.

1. ✔ If Ramón <u>weren't</u> a good father, he (wouldn't worry) so much about Alex.

2. _____ If Alex didn't have a sprained ankle, then Ramón wouldn't need to carry him.

3. _____ Alex would walk if his ankle didn't hurt.

4. _____ If Kevin is interested in Monica, maybe he'll stay in San Francisco.

5. _____ Rebecca would be happy if her brother stayed in San Francisco.

6. _____ Alex wouldn't be at the restaurant tonight if it weren't New Year's Eve.

7. _____ If Ramón weren't so happy, he wouldn't have such a big smile on his face.

8. _____ If Rebecca and Ramón are truly in love, then this will be a very good year.

14. Read each contrary-to-fact conditional sentence. What is the real situation? Circle the letter.

1. If we had time, we'd see a movie.
   a. We'll see a movie.
   b. We don't have time for a movie. *(circled)*

2. I'd help you if I could.
   a. I can't help you.
   b. I can help you.

3. She'd marry him if he asked her.
   a. He asked her to marry him.
   b. He hasn't asked her.

4. If we had the money, we'd buy it.
   a. We can't buy it.
   b. We're going to buy it.

15. Complete the *if* clauses. Use the simple past tense of the verb in parentheses.

1. (be) If we _____ were _____ rich, we'd have a beautiful house.

2. (live) I'd swim every day if I _____ near the beach.

3. (be) If I _____ you, I'd tell them the truth.

4. (have, not) I'd see my friends more if I _____ so much homework.

5. (pay, not) We'd be in trouble if we _____ our bills.

16. Complete the sentences. Write an *if* clause or a result clause. Use your own words.

1. She would get better grades if _she studied every day._____

2. If he were younger, _he'd go out dancing._____

3. If colleges were free, _____

4. If you listened to my advice, _____

5. His parents wouldn't like it if _____

6. Life would be easier if _____

POWER Practice

17. Complete these sentences about you. Write a result clause.

Examples: If I had a great talent, I'd be a great musician.

1. If I were famous, _____

2. If I were the richest person in the world, _____

3. If I knew how to do it, _____

4. If I were the leader of my country, _____